DRAWN TO YOU

A SWEETGUM MEADOWS ROMANCE BOOK 15

IMANI PRICE

Copyright © 2025 by Imani Price
www.ImaniPrice.com

First Edition: December 2025

ISBN 979-8-89283-329-5 (ebook)
ISBN 979-8-89283-330-1 (paperback)

Published by Books to Hook Publishing, LLC.
www.BooksToHook.com

CONTENTS

CHAPTER ONE

The borrowed camera felt foreign in Janelle Brooks's hands as she adjusted the focus on Mrs. Eleanor Washington, who sat in the rocking chair on the wrap-around porch of the Sweetgum Meadows Bed & Breakfast. The afternoon light filtered through the ancient oak trees, creating the kind of golden hour that would have been perfect for her professional rig. Instead, she was working with a basic DSLR her friend William had lent her, knowing it was all she could manage after the incident in Detroit three months ago.

"Now you make sure you get this right, young lady," Mrs. Washington said, though her tone was warm rather than stern. At eighty-three, she had the kind of presence that commanded attention without demanding it. "Rochelle said you specialize in preserving folks' stories, but this biscuit recipe has been in my family since slavery times. Can't write it down proper—it's all in the feel of the dough."

Janelle nodded, grateful that Rochelle Stevens-Walters had not only provided the perfect interview location but had also introduced her to Mrs. Washington. When she'd arrived at the bed and breakfast two days ago, desperate for affordable accommodation and authentic stories, she hadn't expected the owner to become an unofficial community liaison.

"Rochelle tells me you're documenting traditions that might be disappearing," Mrs. Washington continued, settling more comfortably in the rocking chair. "Well, this recipe's been disappearing a little bit with each generation. My great-grandmother passed it to my grandmother, grandmother to my mama, mama to me. But these hands are getting too stiff for the work, and I worry about what happens when I'm gone."

"Can you tell me about the first time you made them yourself?" Janelle asked, pressing record.

Mrs. Washington's eyes softened with memory. "I was eight years old, standing on a wooden crate in my mama's kitchen, watching her hands work that dough like magic. She'd say, 'Ellie, you can't measure love, but you can feel it in the dough.' Took me years to understand what she meant."

The story unfolded like honey, rich and golden, and Janelle found herself genuinely moved rather than calculating its viral potential. Mrs. Washington talked about flour rationed during the Depression, about teaching her own daughters the recipe when they were barely tall enough to reach the counter, about the Sunday mornings when the smell of biscuits would fill the house and draw the whole family to the kitchen.

"These hands," Mrs. Washington said, holding up her weathered fingers, "have made thousands of batches. Fed my babies when they were teething, comforted neighbors during hard times, celebrated every graduation and birthday this family's ever had. Recipe's the same, but every batch tells a different story."

This was why she'd started documenting "America's Hidden Cultural Gems" in the first place—to capture the real stories that mainstream media overlooked. Stories that couldn't be reduced to clickbait headlines or viral moments.

A soft beep from her camera made her heart sink. The battery icon blinked red—again.

"I'm so sorry, Mrs. Washington," Janelle said, lowering the camera. "Could we pause for just a moment?"

"Of course, sugar. These old stories aren't going anywhere."

But Janelle wasn't so sure about that. She fumbled for her backup battery—the last one—knowing it would only give her another thirty minutes tops. The memory hit her like it always did—sudden and sharp. Tammy Johns, twenty-six years old, whose son had been killed in a drive-by shooting. The network had wanted Janelle to keep rolling when the woman collapsed in the courthouse parking lot, sobbing over the verdict. They'd called it "compelling television." Janelle had called it exploitation and turned off her camera.

That night, while she'd been arguing with the producers in the hotel parking lot, someone had smashed her van windows and taken everything. Her Sony FX6, the Rode microphone that could capture every whisper—all gone. Police said it was probably random, but Janelle knew better. Professional equipment didn't just disappear by accident.

Don't think about that, she told herself, snapping the battery into place. *Focus on now.*

"Ready when you are," she said, forcing a smile.

Mrs. Washington continued her story, but Janelle's mind wandered to the envelope in her van. Thirty days. That's how long she had before her storage unit rent was due—the unit holding the few belongings she hadn't sold to afford gas and food. After that, she'd officially have nothing left of her old life except the van she'd been living in and the rapidly dwindling hope that someone, somewhere, would value authentic storytelling over sensationalism.

The interview concluded beautifully, with Mrs. Washington's granddaughter bringing out a plate of the famous biscuits still warm from the oven. Janelle filmed the golden, flaky layers, the butter melting into the soft crumb, the way three generations of women shared the same knowing smile when they bit into them. It was perfect—except for the slight camera shake that her stolen stabilizer would have eliminated.

"Thank you so much," Janelle said, packing her equipment with practiced efficiency. "This will be a beautiful addition to the series."

If there was going to be a series much longer.

Mrs. Washington reached over and patted Janelle's hand. "You've got kind eyes, dear. Don't let whatever's weighing on you steal your light."

Janelle blinked back unexpected tears. "Thank you."

As she finished packing her equipment, Rochelle emerged from the bed and breakfast's front entrance, wiping her hands on a kitchen towel. In her late fifties with silver-streaked hair and the kind of bustling energy that suggested she was always in the middle of three different tasks, Rochelle had the unmistakable air of someone who kept her finger on the pulse of community life.

"How did the interview go?" Rochelle asked, her tone suggesting genuine interest rather than polite inquiry.

"Wonderfully. Mrs. Washington's story about the biscuit

recipe is exactly the kind of cultural preservation I'm trying to document."

"Good, good. Eleanor's got more family history in her head than our local historical society has in their entire archive." Rochelle glanced between them with the assessing look of someone who made connections for a living. "You know, if you're interested in more stories like this, you might want to talk to some of our other longtime residents. There's Mr. Peterson who runs Miller's Hardware Store—his family's been here since the 1920s. And Mrs. Jenkins knows more about the quilting traditions than anyone."

"That would be wonderful," Janelle said, though she wondered how much longer she could afford to stay in Sweetgum Meadows, even with the bed and breakfast's reasonable rates.

"You let me know if you need introductions," Rochelle continued. "This town's got stories that deserve telling, and you seem like someone who'd tell them right."

As Janelle walked back to her converted van parked on Main Street, she reflected on the charm of Sweetgum Meadows with fresh eyes. Founded in 1866 by two freed Black women—Rebecca Johnson and Eleanor Thompson—the town had maintained its character through 150 years of change. White clapboard houses with colorful shutters lined tree-shaded streets. Children rode bicycles on sidewalks where their great-grandparents had played the same games. The town square featured a gazebo where, according to Benjamin Walters at the bed and breakfast, they still held concerts on summer evenings.

The late afternoon air carried the scent of wood smoke and something delicious from Rochelle's Old-Fashioned Diner—Rochelle's Diner to locals—now managed by

Malachi and Aimee. A few doors down, she could see the bright awning of Scoop There It Is ice cream shop, and beyond that, the warm light spilling from Roasted Beans Coffee Spot. It was the kind of Main Street that appeared in movies about small towns, except this one was real, populated by real people with real stories.

This was the kind of place she'd dreamed of belonging to as a kid bouncing between foster homes in Chicago—somewhere with roots, traditions, and people who knew each other's stories. Where Mrs. Washington could sit on her porch and wave to neighbors who'd known her for decades. Where teenagers could walk safely down the street, laughing with their friends without looking over their shoulders.

But she'd learned long ago that she was better at documenting belonging than experiencing it. Safer to stay behind the camera, to observe rather than participate. It was a lesson learned in a dozen different homes with a dozen different families who'd made it clear she was temporary, a visitor who should be grateful for the bed and meals but shouldn't expect to stay.

Her van stood out among the pickup trucks and sedans— a white Ford Transit Connect with Illinois plates and a magnetic sign she'd designed herself: "Real Stories Documentary. Authentic Voices, Authentic Lives." The magnetic letters were starting to peel at the edges, another small reminder of how everything in her life felt temporary these days.

Her phone buzzed. Unknown number.

"Janelle Brooks."

"Ms. Brooks, this is Tracy Wilder from Viral Views Network. I understand you're working on a cultural documentation series?"

Janelle's pulse quickened. She'd sent her pitch to dozens of networks and sponsors over the past month, each rejection feeling like another door closing. "Yes, 'America's Hidden Cultural Gems.' I'm currently filming in Sweetgum Meadows, Georgia."

"Interesting. We're looking for content creators who can deliver authentic stories with broad appeal. However, our audience responds best to conflict and drama. Natural tension, you understand? Can you deliver that?"

The familiar knot formed in Janelle's stomach. She'd heard variations of this conversation too many times. "I focus on authentic community stories. Real people sharing their heritage and traditions. The beauty is in the everyday moments that—"

"Right, but what's the hook? What's the conflict? Are there tensions in this town? Generational disputes? Economic struggles? Young people leaving for the city? Businesses closing? Our viewers need something to keep them engaged, something that makes them feel invested."

Janelle watched a group of elderly men playing checkers outside Rochelle's Diner, their laughter carrying across the street. Rochelle herself was setting up a card table nearby, and Janelle had heard her organizing a book club meeting for later that evening. Where was the conflict in that? Where was the drama in Mrs. Washington's biscuit recipe or the obvious pride Benjamin Walters took in his bed and breakfast?

"I document communities as they are," she said quietly. "Not as entertainment."

"I see. Well, that's probably not a fit for our brand. The market is saturated with feel-good content. People want something with edge, something that makes them feel like they're getting the real story, you know? The stuff people don't want to talk about."

"The real story is usually more beautiful than the manu-factured drama," Janelle said, but she could hear the dismissal in the woman's tone before she even responded.

"That's a lovely sentiment, but it doesn't drive viewership. Good luck with your project."

The line went quiet.

Janelle sat in her van, staring at the phone. That was the fourth rejection this week. At this rate, she'd have to give up the documentary series entirely and find some other way to make a living. Maybe she could wait tables somewhere, save up enough to eventually buy new equipment and start over. But the thought of walking away from the stories that mattered—stories like Mrs. Washington's—felt like losing herself entirely.

A burst of laughter drew her attention across the street. Three teenagers were emerging from a store with a colorful hand-painted sign: "Nerd Central Comics and Video Game Store." The building itself looked like it had been there for decades, with brick walls and large front windows that displayed an array of colorful comic book covers. One of the teens, a tall boy who looked about fifteen, was clutching a comic book like it contained treasure.

"Mr. D said this is the issue where everything changes," he was saying to his friends, his voice carrying the excitement that only comes from discovering something that feels personally meaningful. "Where you see that heroes can look like us."

Janelle found herself reaching for her camera, then stopped. She was supposed to be documenting the historical aspects of Sweetgum Meadows, not random street scenes.

But something about the pure joy on the teenager's face made her reconsider. When was the last time she'd seen a kid that excited about anything that wasn't on a screen?

Through the store's front window, she caught a glimpse of a Black man with graying temples, probably in his early fifties. He was kneeling down to help a younger child reach something on a high shelf, his whole demeanor radiating patience and care. The child, who couldn't have been more than eight or nine, was pointing enthusiastically at something, and even from across the street, she could see the gentle way the man nodded, taking the child's selection seriously.

There was something about the way he moved—gentle authority, like someone who understood that small moments mattered as much as grand gestures. Like someone who knew that making a child feel heard could change their entire day, maybe their entire week.

A bell chimed as the store door opened again, and two more teenagers came out, deep in animated discussion about character development and representation. Their conversation was sophisticated, thoughtful—nothing like the stereotypes about kids who read comics. They were analyzing themes and discussing how stories reflected their own experiences.

Whatever was happening in that store, it clearly meant something to these kids. And the man inside—Mr. D, apparently—seemed to be at the center of it.

Janelle checked her watch. She had about twenty minutes of battery life left, and she'd promised herself she'd use it wisely. Maybe it was worth investigating. This could be exactly the kind of community anchor story her series needed—not the manufactured conflict that Tracy Wilder wanted, but the real connections that made places like Sweetgum Meadows special.

She was halfway across the street, weighing whether to approach the store owner or film the kids' enthusiasm first, when her phone rang again.

A number with a Memphis area code.

"Janelle Brooks."

"This is Lena Price, Harold's neighbor. I've been helping him with arrangements, and he specifically asked me to find someone who'd value his comics—are you the documentary filmmaker who specializes in cultural preservation?"

Janelle stopped walking, nearly stumbling as a car passed by. "Yes, that's me. But I'm not sure how you got my number or—"

"Mr. Murphy is dying, ma'am. He has something called the Black Heroes Longbox—thirty years of Black-led comics and graphic novels. Worth over fifteen thousand dollars, but he's not interested in money. He wants to donate it to someone who will understand its cultural significance and tell its story properly. Someone mentioned you might be interested."

The timing felt like something out of a movie. She was staring at a comic book store, watching teenagers discuss representation, and now someone was calling about a collection of Black superhero comics. "I... I'm flattered, but I'm not a comics expert. I document communities and cultural heritage, but—"

"Ma'am, that's exactly why we're calling. This isn't about being a comics expert. It's about understanding what it means when a kid sees a hero who looks like them. Mr. Murphy spent thirty years collecting these stories because he believes representation matters. He wants the collection to go somewhere it'll be valued and shared with people who need to see themselves as heroes."

Janelle's eyes went back to the comic store, where the man was now visible through the window again, this time showing a small group of kids something behind the counter. Their faces were lit with the same excitement she'd seen on the teenager outside.

"The catch is," Lena continued, "you'd need to get to Memphis by eight PM tomorrow, and you'd need to bring someone who really understands comics—someone who can prove they'd use the collection to help their community, not just for personal gain."

Tomorrow. Eight PM. That was about thirty hours away, and Memphis was roughly an eight-hour drive from Sweetgum Meadows—doable if they left early enough.

"Why the rush?" Janelle asked.

"Mr. Murphy's health is declining rapidly. If no one claims the collection by tomorrow night, it goes to the highest bidder on Monday. Some private collector who'll probably lock it away."

Janelle stared at the comic book store across the street, where the man with gentle authority was now visible through the window, organizing shelves with the same care she'd seen him show the children.

"What exactly would I need to prove?" she asked.

"That you and your partner understand what this collection represents. That you can document its significance and ensure it reaches people who need to see heroes who look like them. Mr. Murphy will test your knowledge and commitment."

A test. With a stranger. For a collection she knew nothing about.

It was exactly the kind of impossible situation that her old self would have walked away from. Too risky, too many variables, too much potential for failure.

But her old self had also had professional equipment, a steady income, and the luxury of being picky about projects.

"I'll need to call you back," she said.

"You have thirty minutes. After that, we're moving to the next name on our list."

The line went dead, leaving Janelle standing in the middle of Main Street with twenty minutes of battery life, thirty dollars in her checking account, and the most improbable opportunity of her career.

She looked back at the comic book store, where the man was now helping the teenage boy from earlier select something from behind the counter. The boy's face lit up like Christmas morning.

Maybe it was time to stop documenting other people's leaps of faith and take one of her own.

Janelle squared her shoulders and walked toward the store, her borrowed camera feeling just a little less foreign in her hands, and the man behind the glass feeling less like a stranger.

CHAPTER TWO

The late afternoon light slanted through the front windows of Nerd Central Comics, casting long shadows across the carefully organized displays that Demetrius Lakeson had spent the better part of fifteen years perfecting. At fifty-two, he could navigate every aisle of his store with his eyes closed, knew exactly which issues were running low, and could recommend the perfect graphic novel for any customer who walked through his door. What he couldn't do, apparently, was figure out how to tell Jerome Washington that they were out of the latest issue of *Storm: Weather Goddess* without disappointing the fifteen-year-old who'd been saving up his allowance for two weeks.

"I'm sorry, Jerome," Demetrius said, checking the delivery schedule on his tablet one more time. "The shipment got delayed. Should be here Thursday morning, and I'll set one aside for you."

Jerome's face fell, but he nodded with the resigned acceptance that came with being a comic book fan in a small town.

"That's okay, Mr. D. Can I look at the back issues while I'm here?"

"Of course. Take your time; first read is for joy." It was something Demetrius had been saying for years, ever since he'd noticed how many young customers rushed through comics like they were homework assignments instead of adventures waiting to unfold.

Jerome wandered toward the back issue bins with the focus of a treasure hunter, and Demetrius returned to his inventory, making notes about which titles were moving faster than expected. Business had been steady lately—not booming, but steady—and he'd learned to be grateful for that. Nerd Central wasn't just a comic book store; it was a gathering place, a safe haven for kids who felt different, and sometimes the only place in town where a fourteen-year-old could talk about the philosophical implications of time travel without getting strange looks.

The bell above the door chimed, and Mrs. Zhang from Sweet and Spicy Chinese Palace down the street poked her head in. "Demetrius, honey, you want your usual order tonight?"

"That sounds perfect, Mrs. Zhang. Thank you."

Jerome appeared at the counter with three back issues of various superhero titles, all featuring Black characters in prominent roles. The boy's selections never failed to make Demetrius proud—and a little heartbroken. When he'd been Jerome's age, finding heroes who looked like him had required dedication and luck. These days, the representation was better, but still not what it should be.

"Good choices," Demetrius said, ringing up the sale. "Have you been keeping up with the *Nubian Knight* series?"

"Yes, sir. I love how they show his day job as a teacher. Makes it feel more real, you know?"

"I do know." Demetrius handed Jerome his change and the bag of comics. "Education is its own superpower."

Jerome grinned and headed for the door, calling back, "See you Thursday for *Storm*!"

The store fell quiet again, leaving Demetrius alone with his thoughts and the familiar comfort of being surrounded by thousands of stories. This was his sanctuary, the place where he'd built something meaningful from scratch. When he'd opened Nerd Central fifteen years ago, people had warned him that a comic book store couldn't survive in a town the size of Sweetgum Meadows. They'd been wrong, but not because of foot traffic or profit margins. The store had survived because it served a need that went deeper than commerce.

His phone buzzed. Text from his sister in Atlanta:

> Still coming to Nyah's graduation party next month? She keeps asking about Uncle D.

He typed back:

> Wouldn't miss it. Tell her I found a first edition of her favorite graphic novel.

> You spoil that child.

> That's my job.

It was easier to be the favorite uncle than to risk being anything more complicated. Safer to pour his energy into other people's families, other people's dreams, than to build something that could be taken away. He'd learned that lesson eight years ago when Denise had packed her bags and moved to Savannah.

"You'll always love this town more than you love any person," she'd said during their final argument. "I can't compete with an entire community, Demetrius. I won't."

He'd tried to explain that loving the community didn't mean he loved her less, that his work at the store was important, that the kids needed him. But she'd been right, in a way. When forced to choose between her demands that he sell the store and move to Savannah with her, and staying in Sweetgum Meadows where he belonged, the choice had been easy. Maybe too easy.

Since then, he'd dated occasionally—dinner with Sarah from the library, a few months with Lisa who taught at the elementary school—but nothing serious. Nothing that required the kind of vulnerability that came with letting someone matter enough to hurt you.

The afternoon customers had thinned out, leaving him with the peaceful routine of closing-day tasks. He was updating his special orders list when a commotion outside caught his attention. Through the front window, he could see three teenagers clustered around Jerome, who was holding up one of his new purchases with obvious excitement.

Demetrius smiled. This was why he did what he did—for moments like this, when a fifteen-year-old kid discovered that heroism came in all colors and that his dreams were valid. It was worth the long hours, the tight margins, and the occasional skepticism from adults who didn't understand why comic books mattered.

Movement across the street caught his eye. A woman with a camera—the documentary filmmaker—was standing beside a white van, watching his store with obvious interest. She was younger than he'd expected, maybe mid-thirties, with natural hair pulled back in a ponytail and an intent expression as she observed the teenagers' animated discussion.

As he watched, she started to cross the street, then stopped when her phone rang. Even from a distance, he could see the conversation was serious—her posture changed, became more tense, and she glanced repeatedly at his store while talking. When the call ended, she stood in the middle of Main Street for a moment, looking conflicted about something.

Then she squared her shoulders and headed directly for Nerd Central.

Demetrius felt his chest tighten. He'd dealt with reporters before—usually when some controversy erupted about comic book content being inappropriate for children, or when a parent complained about the store's influence on their teenager. This woman had the same determined walk, the same focused energy that meant someone was about to ask him questions he didn't want to answer.

He straightened his shoulders and prepared for whatever was coming. After eight years of carefully guarding his heart and fifteen years of protecting his store's reputation, he wasn't about to let some outsider with a camera disrupt the life he'd built.

The bell above the door chimed, and she stepped inside, her camera bag slung over one shoulder and uncertainty flickering across her features. Up close, she was prettier than he'd realized, with intelligent dark eyes and laugh lines that suggested she smiled more often than she worried—though right now, worry seemed to be winning.

"Hi," she said, and her voice had a warm quality that caught him off guard. "I'm Janelle Brooks. I'm working on a documentary about Sweetgum Meadows, and I was wondering... well, hoping, actually... if I could ask you a few questions about your store."

There was something in her tone—not the aggressive confidence he'd expected from a journalist, but something more tentative, almost vulnerable. It threw him off balance.

"Questions about what, specifically?" he asked, keeping his voice carefully neutral.

She glanced around the store, taking in the carefully curated displays, the reading corner with its worn but comfortable chairs, the wall of graphic novels organized by both genre and cultural significance. When her eyes met his again, he saw something he hadn't expected: genuine respect.

"About what you've built here," she said softly. "About what it means to a community when someone creates a space where kids can see themselves as heroes."

The words hit him like a perfectly aimed arrow, finding their mark in the part of his heart he'd thought he'd successfully armored. This wasn't what he'd expected at all.

"Why?" he asked, and realized too late that the question had come out more curious than defensive.

Janelle Brooks took a deep breath, as if she were about to jump off a cliff. "Because I just got a phone call about something called the Black Heroes Longbox, and I think I'm going to need your help."

CHAPTER THREE

The words hung in the air between them like a challenge neither of them had expected. Janelle watched as Demetrius's carefully composed expression shifted from wariness to something that looked almost like recognition—not of her, but of the name she'd just spoken.

"The Black Heroes Longbox," he repeated slowly, and she could hear the capital letters in his voice. "Where did you hear about that?"

"You know what it is?" Relief flooded through her, though she tried not to let it show. She'd been operating on pure instinct since Lena's call, driven by desperation and the cosmic timing of standing outside a comic book store when a stranger offered her the chance of a lifetime.

Demetrius came around the counter, and she noticed he moved with the deliberate care of someone who was used to handling fragile, valuable things. "Every serious collector of Black-led comics knows about Harold Murphy's collection. It's legendary. Thirty years of hunting down first editions, variant covers, signed copies—everything from the mainstream publishers' early attempts at Black superheroes to the indie titles that never got the recognition they deserved."

"So it's real." The relief was stronger now, mixed with something that might have been hope. "The woman who called said it was worth fifteen thousand dollars."

"Conservative estimate," Demetrius said. "If it's everything Harold claims it is, it could be worth twice that. Maybe more." He paused, studying her face. "But Harold Murphy is notoriously particular about who he'll even talk to, let alone sell to. How did you get on his radar?"

Janelle shifted her camera bag to her other shoulder, suddenly aware of how inadequate her equipment must look to someone discussing collections worth thirty thousand dollars. "His neighbor called me. Lena Price. She said he's dying, and he wants to donate the collection to someone who understands its cultural significance. Someone who can tell its story properly."

Something in Demetrius's expression softened, though his posture remained guarded. "Harold's dying?"

"That's what she said. His health is declining rapidly, and if no one claims the collection by tomorrow night, it goes to the highest bidder on Monday." The urgency of it hit her again, that ticking clock that had driven her across the street and through his door. "She said I needed to bring someone who really understands comics. Someone who can prove they'd use the collection to help their community."

"And you thought of me." It wasn't quite a question.

"I saw you through the window with those kids. The way they talked about what you told them, about heroes who look like them..." She gestured toward the store around them, taking in the thoughtful organization, the reading corner, the obvious care that had gone into creating this space. "This isn't just a business for you, is it?"

Demetrius was quiet for a long moment, and she could see him weighing something in his mind. When he spoke, his voice was careful. "What exactly are you proposing, Ms. Brooks?"

"Janelle. And I'm proposing a partnership." The words came out more confidently than she felt. "You have the comics expertise and the community connection. I have the documentary skills to tell the collection's story. Together, we might be able to convince Harold Murphy that we're the right choice."

"And then what? Assuming we somehow pass whatever test Harold has in mind, what happens to the collection?"

This was the part she hadn't fully thought through, the place where her desperation met his obvious skepticism. "I document its significance. You ensure it reaches people who need to see it. We both get what we need."

"Which is?"

"I get the story that saves my career. You get a collection that could transform what you're able to offer this community."

Demetrius walked over to one of his displays, straightening a few comics that didn't need straightening. She recognized the gesture—it was what she did when she needed to think, busying her hands while her mind worked through the implications.

"You said Memphis by tomorrow night. That's about eight hours from here, which means we'd need to leave early morning to have time for whatever Harold wants to put us through."

"So you're considering it?" Hope fluttered in her chest.

He turned back to face her, and she saw the exact moment when his caution gave way to something else—not quite excitement, but a recognition of possibility that matched her own.

"I've been following Harold Murphy's collection for years. Some of those comics... they're pieces of history. Stories that got buried or forgotten because the market wasn't ready for Black heroes, Black creators, Black narratives that went beyond stereotypes." His voice carried a passion that made her understand why those teenagers had looked at him with such respect. "If those stories could find their way here, to these kids..."

"They could see themselves not just as readers, but as part of a tradition," Janelle finished. "Part of a history of representation that goes back decades."

"Exactly." He met her eyes, and she felt that flutter of recognition again—the acknowledgment of someone who understood what mattered to her. "But I need to know what your real intentions are. This isn't just about saving your career, is it?"

The question caught her off guard with its directness. She could have deflected, could have given him the professional answer about cultural preservation and authentic storytelling. Instead, she found herself telling the truth.

"Three months ago, I had everything I thought I wanted. Professional equipment, a growing reputation, opportunities coming from every direction. Then I refused to exploit a grieving mother for content, and it all disappeared overnight." She gestured toward her borrowed camera. "Now I'm living in my van, using equipment held together with hope and determination, documenting communities I can observe but never really belong to."

"And you think this collection will change that?"

"I think this collection represents everything I believe about storytelling. About the power of seeing yourself reflected in the heroes you admire. About preserving culture instead of exploiting it." She took a breath. "And I think if I can help bring it to a community that will value it the way it deserves to be valued, maybe I'll have done something that matters more than likes and views and sponsor deals."

Demetrius was quiet again, but this time the silence felt different—less wary, more considering. When he spoke, his tone had shifted.

"Harold's test won't be easy. He's not just looking for people who know comics. He's looking for people who understand what it means when a kid picks up a comic book and sees a hero who looks like them for the first time. People who understand that representation isn't just about marketing demographics—it's about possibility."

"Can you pass that kind of test?"

"I've been passing it every day for fifteen years," he said simply. "The question is whether we can pass it together."

The bell above the door chimed, and they both turned as Jerome entered with two friends, all three boys stopping short when they saw the intense conversation happening near the counter.

"Sorry, Mr. D," Jerome said. "We can come back later if you're busy."

"Actually," Demetrius said, glancing at Janelle, "you might be able to help us with something. What would it mean to you if this store had access to comics that you couldn't find anywhere else? Stories about heroes who look like you that most people have never even heard of?"

Jerome's eyes lit up. "That would be amazing. Like, life-changing amazing."

"That's what I thought." Demetrius looked back at Janelle. "I'll need to close the store tomorrow, arrange for someone to cover. And we'll need to leave by six AM to make sure we have enough time."

It took her a moment to process what he'd just said. "You're saying yes?"

"I'm saying yes to the collection. The partnership..." He paused, and she saw the flicker of vulnerability he'd been hiding behind all that careful consideration. "We'll figure that out as we go."

Relief and anxiety crashed into each other in her chest. She had a partner. She had a chance. She also had less than twelve hours to prepare for the most important documentary opportunity of her life with a man she'd known for all of twenty minutes.

"There's one more thing," she said, because fairness demanded honesty. "I should probably mention that I'm currently living in my van and have about thirty dollars to my name. So if this partnership involves any expenses..."

"It won't," Demetrius said firmly. "If we're doing this, we're doing it right. I'll handle the travel costs."

"I can't let you—"

"Ms. Brooks. Janelle." His voice carried the same gentle authority she'd observed through the window. "Harold Murphy's collection finding its way to Sweetgum Meadows would be worth far more to this community than whatever it costs to get to Memphis. Let me worry about the logistics."

She nodded, not trusting her voice to stay steady. When was the last time someone had simply taken care of the practical details so she could focus on the work that mattered?

"Six AM," she managed.

"Six AM," he confirmed. "And Janelle? Bring everything you've got. If we're going to convince Harold Murphy that we're the right choice, we're going to need to tell the story of our lives."

CHAPTER FOUR

The parking lot of the Sweetgum Meadows Bed & Breakfast was empty except for Janelle's white van when Demetrius pulled up at five minutes to six. He'd been awake since four-thirty, running through mental checklists and second-guessing every decision that had led him to this moment. In the passenger seat of his SUV sat a thermos of coffee that Mrs. Zhang had insisted on preparing the night before, along with a bag of what she'd called "road trip provisions" that probably contained enough food to feed a small army.

Through the van's front window, he could see Janelle moving around inside, and he wondered if she'd slept at all. The idea of spending the night in a converted van in a strange town would have kept him awake, but then again, she'd been doing it for months. There was a resilience to her that he recognized—the kind that came from having your back against the wall so often that you learned to find footing on the narrowest ledge.

She emerged from the van carrying a worn leather

camera bag and what looked like a small cooler, her hair pulled back in the same practical ponytail she'd worn yesterday. In the early morning light, she looked younger somehow, and he found himself wondering what had driven her to choose a career that required her to be constantly on the move, always documenting other people's homes instead of building her own.

Not your business, he reminded himself. This was a professional arrangement, a way to bring something valuable to his community while helping her get the story she needed. The fact that he'd thought about her more than was strictly necessary while lying awake last night was irrelevant.

"Morning," she said, approaching his SUV. "Thank you for this. I know it's a risk."

"We'll make it work," he said, getting out to help with her equipment. The camera bag was heavier than he'd expected, and he handled it with the same care he used for valuable comics. "Did you get any sleep?"

"Some. You?"

"Some," he echoed, and they shared a smile that acknowledged the shared nervousness neither of them wanted to admit to.

She loaded her things into his backseat while he did a final check of his own supplies. Maps, though his GPS was reliable. Bottled water. The folder of research he'd compiled on Harold Murphy's known collection pieces, cross-referenced with his own knowledge of Black comics history. And, tucked into the side pocket of his overnight bag, a small photo that he wasn't entirely sure why he'd brought.

"Ready?" Janelle asked, settling into the passenger seat.

"Ready," he said, though he wasn't sure he'd ever been less ready for anything in his life.

They drove through downtown Sweetgum Meadows in comfortable silence, past the dark storefronts that would come alive in a few hours. Mrs. Zhang's restaurant sat quietly between Roasted Beans Coffee Spot and the small bookstore, part of the fabric of businesses that made the town feel like a community rather than just a collection of buildings.

"It's beautiful," Janelle said softly as they passed the town square with its gazebo and carefully maintained flower beds. "Even at this hour, you can feel how much people care about this place."

"It gets in your blood," Demetrius agreed. "I left for college thinking I'd never come back, that I needed something bigger, more exciting. Took me about a semester to realize that bigger isn't always better."

"What made you realize that?"

He considered the question as they reached the highway and he merged into the sparse early morning traffic. "Loneliness, mostly. In a city, you can be surrounded by thousands of people and still feel completely alone. Here, Mrs. Zhang notices if I don't order dinner on my usual night. Jerome stops by to check on me if I seem stressed. It's the difference between existing and belonging."

Janelle was quiet for a moment, and when he glanced over, she was staring out the passenger window at the Georgia countryside beginning to wake up in the early light.

"I've been documenting communities like yours for five years," she said finally. "Places where people belong to something bigger than themselves. And I've never experienced it myself."

"Never? Not growing up?"

"Foster care." The words came out matter-of-fact, but he

caught the slight tightening around her eyes. "Twelve different homes between the ages of eight and eighteen. You learn not to get too attached to places or people."

"That must have been hard." The understatement felt inadequate, but he sensed she wouldn't appreciate pity.

"It was what it was. But it's why I do what I do now, I think. Documenting the connections I've never had, trying to understand how some people make it look so easy."

"It's not easy," Demetrius said. "Community takes work. It takes showing up, even when you don't feel like it. It takes caring about people who might disappoint you."

"Is that hard for you? The caring part, I mean?"

The question surprised him with its directness, though he supposed it shouldn't have. Documentary filmmakers were probably trained to ask the questions that mattered, not just the comfortable ones.

"Sometimes. I had someone once who wanted me to choose between caring about the community and caring about her. My ex-wife." He adjusted his grip on the steering wheel. "She said I'd never love any person as much as I loved that town."

"Were you able to prove her wrong?"

"I chose the town," he said quietly. "So I guess she was right."

They drove in silence for a while after that, the landscape gradually changing from small towns to farmland to the suburbs that surrounded larger cities. Demetrius found himself stealing glances at Janelle, noting the way she absently twisted her hair when she was thinking, the careful attention she paid to everything they passed.

"Can I ask you something?" she said eventually.

"Sure."

"Yesterday, when you were helping that little girl reach the comic book, what did you say to her?"

He thought back to the afternoon before, which felt like a lifetime ago. "Probably something about taking her time, that the first read should be for joy. Why?"

"It's just... I was watching from across the street, and there was something about the way you interacted with her. Like you understood that what she was choosing mattered."

"It does matter. Comics were my first window into worlds where anything was possible, where problems could be solved and heroes came in all shapes and sizes." He slowed for a construction zone, using the pause to organize his thoughts. "That little girl was picking out her first graphic novel. In ten years, she might be creating her own stories because of what she discovered yesterday."

"That's a lot of faith to place in a comic book."

"Stories shape us," Demetrius said simply. "The ones we tell ourselves, the ones we read, the ones we choose to believe about what's possible. If I can help kids in Sweetgum Meadows find stories that expand their idea of what's possible, then I've done something worthwhile."

An hour into their drive, Janelle opened her small cooler and pulled out what looked like homemade granola bars and fruit. "Mrs. Washington packed these for me yesterday after our interview. Said I looked like I needed feeding."

"That sounds like her. She's been mothering the whole town for as long as I can remember." He accepted one of the granola bars gratefully. "What did you think of her story? The biscuit recipe?"

"It was beautiful. The idea that some knowledge can't be written down, that it has to be passed hand to hand, heart to heart." Janelle took a bite of an apple, chewing thoughtfully. "That's what you're doing with those kids, isn't it? Passing along something that can't be reduced to a lesson plan."

"I hadn't thought about it that way, but yes. The love of stories, the understanding that representation matters, the confidence to see yourself as the hero of your own narrative —those aren't things you can teach with a textbook."

"And that's what Harold's collection represents to you. More tools for that kind of teaching."

"Exactly." He felt a familiar spark of excitement at the thought. "Some of those comics... they're pieces of history that most people have never seen. Stories about Black characters that go beyond stereotypes, that show complexity and heroism and humanity. If I could share those with Jerome, with the other kids who come into the store..."

"They'd see that they're part of a longer tradition of representation."

"Right. That the heroes who look like them aren't new, they've just been overlooked or forgotten." He glanced at her, saw the same enthusiasm in her eyes that he felt. "That's the story you want to tell, isn't it? Not just about the collection, but about what it means."

"I want to tell the story about what happens when kids see themselves reflected in the heroes they admire. About what changes when representation becomes more than just a marketing buzzword." She closed her notebook, which had been open on her lap. "I want to show what you already know—that stories matter."

They stopped for gas and coffee at a rest area two hours into the drive. While Demetrius filled the tank, Janelle wandered over to a picnic table where she pulled out her borrowed camera and started filming the early morning travelers, the truckers stretching their legs, the families corralling sleepy children.

"What are you capturing?" he asked when he joined her.

"The in-between moments. The transition from one place to another, one story to another." She lowered the camera, looking slightly embarrassed. "Probably nothing usable, but sometimes the best footage comes from unexpected moments."

"Can I see?"

She hesitated, then handed him the camera, showing him how to review the footage. The shots were simple but compelling—a father lifting a toddler to see over a fence, an elderly couple sharing coffee from the same cup, a trucker helping a stranded motorist with jumper cables.

"These are wonderful," he said, meaning it. "You have an eye for the moments that reveal character."

"Thank you." She took the camera back, her fingers brushing his briefly. "I used to have better equipment for this kind of work, but the borrowed camera is teaching me to be more intentional about what I capture."

"Sometimes limitations force creativity."

"That's what I keep telling myself."

Back on the road, their conversation turned to comics history, and Demetrius found himself sharing stories he rarely told—about the first comic that made him cry, about the characters who'd shaped his understanding of heroism, about the creators who'd fought to tell authentic stories in an industry that wasn't always ready to hear them.

"There was this one comic," he said as they crossed into Tennessee. "1979, small publisher, almost nobody bought it. It was about a Black superhero who was also a social worker in Detroit. The stories weren't about fighting cosmic threats or saving the universe. They were about protecting kids from abusive homes, about fighting systemic racism, about being a hero in the real world."

"What happened to it?"

"Canceled after eight issues. The publisher said there wasn't a market for that kind of story." He shook his head. "But Harold Murphy has all eight issues in mint condition. I read in an interview once that he drove to three different states to find issue number seven."

"And now those stories could end up in your store."

"If we can convince him we deserve them."

The morning sun was getting higher, and the traffic was getting heavier as they approached Nashville. Janelle had been quiet for the past few miles, staring out the window with a thoughtful expression.

"Can I tell you something?" she said suddenly.

"Of course."

"I'm scared." The words came out in a rush. "Not just about Harold's test, but about what happens if we actually succeed. I've been running for so long, moving from story to story, that I'm not sure I know how to build anything that lasts."

"What's scary about building something?"

"Disappointing people. Having them get to know me well enough to decide I'm not worth the investment." She twisted her hair nervously. "It's easier to be the person with the camera who shows up, captures the story, and leaves before anyone expects too much."

Demetrius was quiet for a moment, processing the vulnerability in her admission. "You know, when I decided to open the store, everyone told me I was crazy. Small-town comic shop, limited customer base, no guaranteed income. They weren't wrong about the risks."

"But you did it anyway."

"I did it anyway. And you know what I learned? Sometimes the scariest risks are the ones worth taking most." He merged around a slower car, giving himself time to choose his words carefully. "Building something that matters is always scary because it means you have something to lose. But it also means you have something worth protecting."

"Like what?"

"Like letting people get to know you well enough to decide you're worth fighting for."

She was quiet for a long time after that, and he wondered if he'd said too much. But when she finally spoke, her voice was softer than before.

"When I was sixteen, I had a foster family that I thought might be different. The Hendersons. They had two biological kids and they treated me like... like I belonged. For eight months, I believed I'd finally found my place."

"What happened?"

"Budget cuts. The state reduced the stipend for older foster kids, and the Hendersons couldn't afford to keep me." She stared out the window. "They cried when they told me. Said it broke their hearts. But I still had to leave."

"That wasn't about you not being worth keeping."

"I know that now. But at sixteen, all I understood was that I wasn't worth the financial sacrifice. So I learned not to need that kind of belonging." She looked at him. "Your ex-wife, when she gave you the ultimatum about the store—part of you must have understood why she needed you to choose."

The observation was astute and uncomfortable. "I understood it, but I couldn't do it. The store wasn't just a business to me. It was how I served something bigger than myself."

"And she wanted to be bigger than the store."

"She wanted to be the only thing that mattered to me. But I couldn't understand why loving her had to mean abandoning everything else I cared about." He was quiet for a moment. "Maybe we were just incompatible. She needed someone who could make her the center of their universe, and I needed someone who understood that my community work was part of who I was."

"That doesn't sound like a character flaw on either side. Just different needs."

"I used to think it was my fault for not being able to give her what she needed. But you're right - we just wanted different things from a relationship."

"Unknown number," she said, checking the display. "Should I answer?"

"Might be Harold or Lena."

She answered, putting it on speaker. "Janelle Brooks."

"Ms. Brooks, this is Lena Price. I wanted to check that you're still coming today. Harold's been asking about you and your partner."

"We're on our way. Should be there by early afternoon."

"Good. I should warn you, he's been... particular about the arrangements. He wants to meet in his apartment rather than somewhere public, and he's prepared what he calls a comprehensive evaluation."

Demetrius and Janelle exchanged glances.

"We'll be ready," Demetrius said.

"I hope so. Harold Murphy doesn't give second chances."

The call ended, and they drove in thoughtful silence for several miles.

"Comprehensive evaluation," Janelle said finally.

"We knew it wouldn't be simple."

"Are you worried?"

Demetrius considered the question honestly. "Yes. But not about our knowledge or our intentions. I'm worried about whether we can convince him that Sweetgum Meadows is the right home for thirty years of his life's work."

"What would convince you, if you were in his position?"

"Proof that the collection wouldn't just sit on shelves. That it would be shared, used, valued by people who need to see those stories." He glanced at her. "And proof that the people asking for it understand the difference between cultural preservation and cultural exploitation."

"Then that's what we show him."

By the time they reached the outskirts of Memphis, it was nearly 2 PM, and they were both feeling the effects of the long drive. The reality of what they were attempting was settling over them both. In a few hours, they'd be sitting across from Harold Murphy, trying to convince him they deserved thirty years of his life's work.

"Ready for this?" Demetrius said as they pulled into the parking lot of Harold Murphy's apartment complex.

Janelle gathered her notes and camera bag. "As ready as we can be, I think."

"Whatever his test involves, we stick to what we know. The collection's cultural significance, how it could serve the community." He turned off the engine. "We're here for the right reasons."

"Agreed." She opened her door. "Let's go convince Harold Murphy we deserve thirty years of his life's work."

The apartment building was older than Janelle had expected, probably built in the 1970s with that particular shade of brick that seemed designed to blend into the background. But the grounds were well-maintained, with small flower beds that showed someone cared about keeping the place welcoming. A small sign by the entrance indicated that apartments 1A through 1D were on the ground floor—perfect accessibility for elderly residents.

"Apartment 1B," Demetrius said, stopping in front of a door painted forest green at the end of the ground floor hallway. Before either of them could knock, the door opened to reveal a woman in her sixties with silver-streaked hair pulled back in a neat bun.

"You must be Ms. Brooks and Mr. Lakeson," she said, her voice carrying the warm authority of someone accustomed to taking care of details. "I'm Lena Price. Harold's been waiting for you."

She stepped back to let them enter, and Janelle was immediately struck by the apartment's atmosphere. Every available wall space was covered with carefully framed comic book covers, but these weren't the chaotic collections of an obsessive fan. They were curated displays that told stories—progression of art styles, evolution of characters, milestones in representation. It was like walking into a museum designed by someone who understood that comics were literature, not just entertainment.

"He's set up in the living room today," Lena said quietly, her voice taking on a more subdued tone. "He's having a good day—alert and determined to meet with you—but please keep in mind that he tires easily."

As they followed her down a short hallway, Janelle noticed the subtle modifications throughout the apartment—grab bars installed along the walls, a wheelchair folded in the corner, and the unmistakable smell of medical supplies that always seemed to linger in spaces where someone was fighting a losing battle against illness.

The living room had been converted into a makeshift bedroom, with a hospital bed positioned to face the large windows that looked out onto a small courtyard garden. Harold Murphy was propped up against several pillows, an oxygen cannula beneath his nose and two wheeled tray tables positioned on either side of his bed within easy reach. What struck Janelle most was how small he looked in the mechanical bed—probably no more than five-foot-six even when standing, but now appearing almost fragile beneath the crisp white sheets.

Yet his dark eyes held the same sharp intelligence she'd expected, and when his gaze settled on her, she felt as though he was reading her entire professional history. The tray tables were covered with plastic sleeves, each containing what she assumed were comics, organized into neat rows that Harold could reach without straining.

"Ms. Brooks. Mr. Lakeson." His voice was softer than she'd imagined, a little breathless, but determined. "Thank you for making the drive. I know it wasn't a small commitment."

"Thank you for considering us," Demetrius replied, and Janelle could hear the genuine respect in his voice, now tempered with obvious concern for Harold's condition. "Your collection is legendary in the community."

Harold's mouth quirked in what might have been a smile, though the effort seemed to cost him. "Legendary is one word for it. My late wife called it an expensive obsession." His expression softened briefly. "She understood, though. Understood why these stories mattered enough to hunt down."

Lena quietly arranged two chairs beside the bed, close enough for conversation but positioned so Harold wouldn't have to strain to see them.

"How long have you been collecting?" Janelle asked, pulling out her notebook. The documentary instinct was automatic, but she also genuinely wanted to understand the man who'd spent thirty years building something this significant.

"Officially? Since 1993." Harold paused to take a slightly deeper breath, the oxygen cannula clearly helping. "That's when I bought my first comic specifically because it featured a Black superhero who wasn't a stereotype. Unofficially, I've been thinking about representation in comics since I was twelve years old and realized that none of the heroes I was reading looked like me or dealt with problems that felt familiar."

He gestured weakly toward the tray tables covered with comics. "Before we talk about the collection," he continued, his voice gaining strength as he focused on his purpose, "I need to understand what you think you're asking for. Lena tells me you want to document the cultural significance of these comics, Ms. Brooks, and that you want to make them available to your community, Mr. Lakeson."

"That's right," Demetrius said carefully, clearly adjusting his approach to Harold's fragile state.

Harold's breathing became slightly more labored, and Lena moved closer to the bed, checking the oxygen flow. "Take your time, Harold," she said gently.

"I'm fine," he insisted, though he accepted the small cup of water she offered. After a sip, he continued. "You're both wrong. You're not asking me to document anything or make anything available. You're asking me to trust you with thirty years of my life. You're asking me to believe that you'll treat these stories with the respect they deserve, not because of their monetary value, but because of what they represent."

The weight of his words settled over the room like a sacred charge. Janelle glanced at Demetrius and saw her own sudden nervousness reflected in his eyes, magnified now by the reality of Harold's condition. This wasn't going to be a simple transaction or even a friendly conversation about shared interests. This was a dying man's final act of cultural preservation, and they were being asked to carry that torch.

"You're right," Janelle said carefully. "We are asking for your trust. But we're also offering ours. We're trusting that you want these stories to continue reaching people who need them, not sit in someone's private collection gathering dust."

Harold leaned back against his pillows, the small movement clearly requiring effort. "Tell me about your documentary work, Ms. Brooks. What kinds of stories do you usually tell?"

The question felt like a test within a test, and Janelle was acutely aware of the oxygen machine's quiet hum in the background, marking time that Harold didn't have to waste. She could give him the professional answer, the elevator pitch she'd used with potential sponsors. Or she could tell him the truth about why she'd chosen this particular form of storytelling.

"I document communities," she said. "Places where people have maintained connections and traditions despite pressure to change or disappear. I'm interested in how people preserve culture authentically, not how they package it for outsiders."

"And what's the difference?" Harold's voice was getting softer, but his focus remained intense.

"Authentic preservation serves the community first. It's about maintaining traditions and stories because they matter to the people who live with them. Packaging culture for outsiders is about making it palatable and marketable to people who don't need to understand it deeply."

Harold nodded slowly, the effort clearly tiring him. "Give me an example."

Janelle thought about the various communities she'd documented, aware that Harold was using precious energy for this conversation.

"Two years ago, I was documenting a Native American community in New Mexico. They had traditional pottery techniques that had been passed down for generations, and there was concern that younger people weren't learning them. The tribal council wanted me to focus on the artistic beauty, the cultural uniqueness, the tourist appeal of the pottery."

"But?" Harold prompted, though his breathing had become more shallow.

"But when I spent time with the potters, I learned that the techniques weren't just about making beautiful objects. They were about meditation, community connection, spiritual practice. The pottery was the outcome, but the process was what mattered to the community. So that's what I documented—the process, the relationships, the meaning behind the techniques, not just the products."

Harold closed his eyes for a moment, and Lena stepped forward in concern, but he waved her back gently. "And how did that go over with your sponsors?" he asked without opening his eyes.

Janelle felt heat rise in her cheeks. "They didn't renew my contract. Said the story lacked commercial appeal."

For the first time since they'd arrived, Harold smiled—a genuine expression that transformed his entire face despite his obvious fatigue. "Good. That means you made the right choice." He opened his eyes and turned to Demetrius with visible effort. "Your turn, Mr. Lakeson. Tell me about your comic store. What makes it different from ordering comics online?"

Demetrius leaned forward slightly, speaking more softly than usual as if he understood that Harold was conserving strength for what mattered most. "Online, comics are products. In my store, they're conversations. When Jerome comes in looking for stories about characters who look like him, we don't just talk about which issues to buy. We talk about representation, about seeing yourself as a hero, about how stories shape the way we think about what's possible."

Harold's breathing had become more labored, but his attention remained focused. "You think comics can change how kids see themselves?"

"I know they can. I've watched it happen." Demetrius's voice carried quiet conviction. "Three months ago, a little girl came into the store with her grandmother. Eight years old, maybe nine. She'd never read a comic book before, wasn't sure she wanted to try. Her grandmother convinced her to pick just one."

Harold was listening intently now, though Lena had moved to adjust his pillows to help with his breathing.

"What did she choose?" Harold asked, his voice barely above a whisper.

"A story about a young Black girl who discovers she has the power to heal plants, to make things grow. Simple premise, but the execution was beautiful. The character dealt with self-doubt, with feeling different from her classmates, with learning to see her differences as strengths instead of problems."

Harold's eyes had closed again, but Janelle could see he was still listening.

"Two weeks later," Demetrius continued, "she came back for the next issue. A month after that, she was reading everything she could find with strong female characters. Last week, her grandmother told me the girl has started writing her own stories."

Harold opened his eyes, and despite his obvious exhaustion, they held a spark of recognition. "And you think my collection would expand those possibilities?"

"I think your collection would show kids like Jerome and that little girl that they're part of a long tradition of representation. That Black heroes in comics aren't new or trendy

—they're part of a history that goes back decades, created by people who understood the importance of seeing yourself in the stories that matter to you."

Harold was quiet for a long moment, his breathing the only sound in the room. When he finally spoke, his voice was so soft they had to lean closer to hear him.

"Thirty years," he whispered. "Thirty years of hunting down stories that other people overlooked or dismissed. Driving to three states to find a single issue. Paying more than I could afford because I knew that if I didn't preserve these stories, they might disappear entirely."

He looked toward the window, where the afternoon light was beginning to fade. "My wife died two years ago. Cancer." His voice caught slightly on the word. "Before she passed, she made me promise that the collection wouldn't end up gathering dust in some collector's basement or being sold piece by piece to whoever would pay the most. She said these stories deserved to keep changing lives."

The room was completely quiet except for the soft hum of the oxygen machine and the tick of a clock somewhere in the kitchen.

"So here's what we're going to do," Harold continued, his voice gaining a final surge of strength. "I'm going to show you twenty comics from my collection. Not the most valuable ones, not the rarest ones, but twenty that represent the breadth and depth of what I've been preserving. You're going to tell me what you see in them—not their market value, not their publication history, but their cultural significance. What story they tell about representation, about progress, about the ongoing fight to see Black characters as fully human heroes."

Janelle felt her heart rate increase. This was it—the test

that would determine whether months of desperation and a single day of partnership would lead to the opportunity that could change both of their lives. And they were asking a dying man to use what might be some of his final hours to evaluate their worthiness.

"If you can convince me that you understand what these comics represent," Harold said, his hand trembling slightly as he reached for the first plastic sleeve on the tray table to his right, "then we'll talk about the collection finding a home in Sweetgum Meadows. If you can't..." He shrugged weakly. "Then you'll have had a nice drive to Memphis, and the collection will go to auction on Monday."

He held up the first comic with visible effort, and Janelle felt the weight of everything that had led to this moment settle around them like a challenge waiting to be met.

"Are you ready?" Harold asked, his voice barely audible but his eyes still sharp with purpose.

Janelle looked at Demetrius, saw her own mixture of excitement and terror reflected in his eyes. They'd spent eight hours talking about comics, culture, and community, but this was where they'd discover whether they truly understood what Harold Murphy had spent his life preserving.

"We're ready," she said, opening her notebook to a fresh page and hoping they were about to prove worthy of a dying man's final act of faith.

CHAPTER SIX

The first comic Harold held up was in a pristine plastic sleeve, but Demetrius could see immediately that it wasn't one of the mainstream titles he was familiar with. The cover showed a Black woman in a flowing white dress standing in what looked like a hospital room, her hands glowing with golden light as she tended to a child in a bed. The art style was sophisticated, with muted colors that suggested this was from the late 1980s or early 1990s.

"*Healing Hands* number one, 1989," Harold said, his voice barely above a whisper but still carrying authority. "Independent publisher called Urban Stories. Tell me what you see."

Demetrius studied the cover more carefully, aware that this wasn't about identifying publishing details or market value. This was about understanding what the comic represented in the broader context of Black representation in comics.

"I see a Black woman as the central figure," he said slowly. "Not a sidekick, not comic relief, but the hero. And her power isn't about violence or aggression—it's about healing, about nurturing. The hospital setting suggests she's working within existing systems to help people, not standing apart from society."

Harold nodded slightly, though the effort seemed to tire him. "What else?"

Janelle leaned forward, studying the comic alongside Demetrius. "The way she's positioned in the frame—she's confident, professional. The child in the bed is looking up at her with trust, not fear. This isn't about a mysterious, other-worldly figure. This is about competence and care."

"The dress," Demetrius added, seeing it now. "It's white, but it's not a typical superhero costume. It looks profes-sional, like she could be a doctor or nurse. The golden glow around her hands is the only thing that marks her as having powers."

Harold's breathing had become more labored, but his eyes remained focused. "Good. Now tell me why that mattered in 1989."

Demetrius felt the weight of the question. He knew enough about comics history to understand that 1989 was still early in terms of meaningful Black representation in the medium, especially for Black women who weren't defined by trauma or stereotypes.

"In 1989, most Black characters in comics were either part of teams where they filled a diversity slot, or they were urban vigilantes dealing with drugs and violence," he said. "A Black woman with healing powers, working in a professional medical setting, would have been revolutionary. She's not defined by suffering or anger. Her power comes from a desire to help, and she's working within society, not outside it."

"And the publishing context?" Harold asked, though his voice was getting weaker.

"Independent publisher," Janelle said. "Which means this story existed outside the mainstream industry. Someone believed in this character enough to create her, fund her publication, and get her to market without corporate backing. This represents the kind of grassroots representation that was happening beneath the surface of mainstream comics."

Harold smiled slightly, the first genuine expression of approval they'd seen from him. "Exactly. *Healing Hands* ran for sixteen issues before Urban Stories went bankrupt. The character was ahead of her time." He set the comic aside carefully and reached for another one. "Most collectors have never heard of her, but she influenced a generation of creators who remembered that Black heroes could be healers instead of warriors."

The second comic showed a young Black boy, maybe twelve years old, floating cross-legged in the air above a city street. He was wearing ordinary clothes—jeans, sneakers, a red t-shirt—and reading a book while various urban scenes played out below him. The art style was more recent, probably from the mid-2000s.

"*Street Scholar* number seven, 2004," Harold said. "Dante James, age twelve, has the power of flight but uses it mainly to find quiet places to read. Tell me about the choices the creators made."

This one felt more familiar to Demetrius, closer to his experience with the kids who came into his store. "They made him ordinary," he said. "His power is incredible—flight —but he's not using it to fight crime or save the world. He's using it to escape the noise and chaos so he can read in peace."

"The book," Janelle added, pointing to the volume in the character's hands. "It looks substantial, not a comic book or graphic novel. This kid is serious about learning."

"And the street scene below him," Demetrius continued. "It's urban, but it's not stereotypically dangerous. There are families walking, people going about their business. He's not escaping from danger—he's escaping to find the quiet he needs to think."

Harold nodded, though the movement seemed to cost him energy. "What does that say about how young Black boys are typically portrayed in media?"

The question was pointed, and Demetrius felt the weight of it. "Usually, young Black boys in comics are either victims of their environment—dealing with violence, poverty, family trauma—or they're defined by athletic ability or street smarts. This character is defined by intellectual curiosity. His superpower gives him the freedom to pursue learning on his own terms."

"The solitude is a choice, not isolation imposed by others," Janelle observed. "He has agency over his own environment."

"Right," Harold whispered. "And the fact that he's twelve years old..."

"It shows Black intellectual curiosity as natural and inherent, not something that has to be developed despite obstacles," Demetrius finished. "This kid doesn't have to overcome his environment to be smart. He just needs space to let his intelligence flourish."

Harold's hand trembled slightly as he set the second comic aside. Lena moved closer to adjust his pillows, and for a moment, Demetrius thought the session might be over. But Harold waved her back gently and reached for a third comic.

This cover was darker, more dramatic. A Black man in his thirties stood in what looked like a courtroom, wearing a business suit but with his hands glowing with some kind of energy. Behind him, shadowy figures in judicial robes seemed to be recoiling from his presence.

"*Justice Served* number twelve, 1995," Harold said, his voice growing weaker but maintaining its focus. "Lawyer by day, but his powers only work when someone is lying in his presence. What's the significance?"

Demetrius studied the image, thinking about the implications. "He's working within the legal system, not outside it. His power doesn't make him judge and jury—it just reveals truth. The people in robes are recoiling because they're corrupt, not because he's threatening violence."

"The business suit," Janelle added. "He's professional, educated, respectable. But the glowing hands suggest his power makes some people uncomfortable, even when he's on the side of justice."

"The courtroom setting is crucial," Demetrius continued. "This isn't about vigilante justice or taking the law into his own hands. This is about using extraordinary abilities to make existing systems work better, to serve justice rather than replace it."

Harold closed his eyes for a moment, his breathing becoming more shallow. When he opened them again, his gaze was intense despite his obvious fatigue.

"All three of these comics," he said slowly, "represent something that was rare when they were published and is still rare today. Black characters whose powers serve their communities, whose abilities are used constructively rather than destructively, who work within society rather than standing apart from it."

He paused, seeming to gather strength. "They're not origin stories about overcoming trauma. They're not revenge fantasies. They're not about proving worthiness to white institutions. They're about Black characters who have power and use it to build rather than tear down."

Demetrius felt something shift in his understanding, not just of these specific comics but of what Harold had been preserving for three decades. "You weren't just collecting Black characters," he said slowly. "You were collecting positive representations of Black power."

"Power used responsibly," Janelle added. "Power that serves community rather than individual ego."

Harold smiled again, though the effort was clearly enormous. "Now you're beginning to understand," he whispered. "These aren't just comics about Black heroes. They're comics about what Black heroism could look like when it's not defined by white narratives about Black trauma."

He set the third comic aside and looked at both of them with eyes that seemed to hold thirty years of careful curation. "I have seventeen more to show you," he said. "But first, I need to know—if these stories found their way to your community, Mr. Lakeson, how would you use them?"

The question hung in the air like a final exam, and Demetrius realized that everything—Janelle's career, his store's future impact, Harold's dying wish—depended on his answer being not just correct, but authentic.

"I wouldn't just put them on shelves," he said carefully. "I'd use them to start conversations. When Jerome comes in looking for heroes who look like him, I'd show him that Black heroes have been using their powers constructively for decades. When that little girl comes back looking for more stories about girls like her, I'd show her a tradition of Black women using extraordinary abilities to heal and build."

Harold's breathing was becoming more labored, but he gestured for Demetrius to continue.

"I'd create displays that show the progression of representation, help kids understand they're part of an ongoing story, not just readers of individual comics. And I'd make sure other comic store owners knew about these titles, help get them reprinted if possible."

"And the documentation?" Harold asked, turning his weary gaze to Janelle.

"I'd tell the story of what you preserved and why it mattered," she said. "Not just the individual comics, but the act of preservation itself. The story of someone who spent thirty years ensuring that positive Black representation in comics wouldn't be lost or forgotten."

Harold closed his eyes again, and this time the silence stretched longer. Lena stepped forward, checking his breathing, but he raised one weak hand to indicate he was still present.

When he opened his eyes again, there was something different in his expression—not the evaluation of a test-giver, but the recognition of someone who had found what he was looking for.

"Show me the next seventeen," he whispered. "I think you're ready to see what thirty years of hope looks like."

CHAPTER SEVEN

The next hour passed in a blur of carefully preserved stories, each comic Harold showed them revealing another facet of the vision he'd been curating for thirty years. Janelle found herself taking notes not just about the individual titles, but about the patterns emerging from Harold's choices—the consistent thread of Black characters using extraordinary abilities to build rather than destroy, to heal rather than harm, to work within communities rather than stand apart from them.

Harold's strength was clearly waning. Lena had to help him hold some of the later comics, and his explanations became shorter, more breathless. But his focus never wavered, and with each title he presented, Janelle understood more deeply what they were being entrusted with.

Urban Guardian from 1997 featured a Black woman who could manipulate technology, but instead of being a cyber-warrior, she used her abilities to bridge the digital divide in her neighborhood, teaching elderly residents how to use computers and helping small businesses get online. *Community Voices* from 2001 centered on a teenage boy whose telepathic abilities helped him mediate conflicts between gangs, facilitating communication rather than choosing sides.

"These aren't power fantasies," Janelle said during a brief pause while Lena adjusted Harold's oxygen flow. "They're responsibility fantasies. Characters who have extraordinary abilities but use them in ordinary, constructive ways."

Harold nodded weakly. "That's exactly what they are," he whispered. "And that's exactly why most of them failed commercially. Publishers wanted conflict, wanted drama, wanted heroes who fought clear villains. These characters solved problems through communication and community building."

The seventeenth comic was *Neighborhood Watch* from 2003, featuring an older Black man whose power was enhanced perception—he could see and hear everything happening in a six-block radius. But instead of using this for surveillance or crime fighting, he used it to coordinate community responses to problems: knowing when elderly neighbors needed help, when teenagers were struggling and needed mentorship, when small disputes were escalating before they became serious conflicts.

"He's like a one-man social services department," Demetrius observed. "Using superhuman abilities to do what community organizers and social workers do every day, just more efficiently."

"Exactly," Harold said, his voice barely audible now. "And the comic ran for only eight issues because readers couldn't connect with a hero whose biggest victories were preventing problems before they happened."

He set the final comic aside and looked at both of them with eyes that seemed to hold decades of hope and disappointment. The afternoon light from the window had shifted, casting longer shadows across the room, and Janelle realized they'd been there for nearly two hours.

"Those are twenty comics out of more than three hundred in the complete collection," Harold said. "Every single one represents a choice to preserve stories that the market rejected but that communities needed. Stories that showed Black characters as builders, healers, teachers, mediators. Stories that imagined Black power as fundamentally constructive rather than reactive."

Lena approached the bed with a concerned expression. "Harold, you need to rest. Your breathing—"

"I'm fine," he insisted, though clearly he wasn't. "I need to finish this."

He turned back to Janelle and Demetrius, his gaze intense despite his obvious exhaustion. "Here's what I need to know before we go any further. Ms. Brooks, you've documented communities and their cultural preservation efforts. But this collection isn't just about preserving culture—it's about preserving hope. These comics imagined better versions of what Black heroism could look like. If you tell their story, can you help people understand that distinction?"

The question went to the heart of everything Janelle had been struggling with in her career. "Yes," she said simply. "Because that's what authentic cultural preservation is really about—not just maintaining traditions, but maintaining the vision and hope that created those traditions in the first place."

Harold smiled, the expression transforming his exhausted

face. "And Mr. Lakeson, your store serves as a gathering place for young people who need to see themselves reflected in heroic narratives. If these comics found their way to Sweetgum Meadows, could you help your community understand that Black heroism doesn't have to be defined by trauma or reaction to oppression?"

Demetrius was quiet for a moment, and Janelle could see him thinking not just about his answer, but about the responsibility Harold was offering them. "I think that's exactly what my community needs to understand," he said finally. "These kids—Jerome, that little girl with her grandmother—they're not looking for heroes who have overcome the same struggles they face. They're looking for heroes who show them what's possible when you have power and choose to use it constructively."

"They need to see that their power—their intelligence, their creativity, their capacity for community building—that these are heroic qualities, not just coping mechanisms," Janelle added.

Harold closed his eyes, and for a moment, the only sound in the room was the quiet hum of the oxygen machine. When he opened them again, there was something different in his expression—a kind of peace that hadn't been there before.

"Lena," he said softly. "Get the paperwork."

Janelle felt her heart skip. "Harold—"

"You've convinced me," he said, his voice gaining a final surge of strength. "Not just that you understand what these comics represent, but that you understand why that representation matters. You've shown me that you see the difference between preserving artifacts and preserving vision."

Lena returned with a manila folder, her own eyes bright with what looked like relief and sadness mixed together.

"The collection is yours," Harold said to both of them. "All three hundred and twelve comics, along with the research notes I've compiled over thirty years about creators, publication histories, and cultural impact. Ms. Brooks, I want you to document not just the collection, but the philosophy behind it. Help people understand that positive representation isn't just nice to have—it's necessary for communities to envision better versions of themselves."

He paused, breathing heavily. "And Mr. Lakeson, I want these stories to live in your community, not just sit on shelves. I want kids in Sweetgum Meadows to understand that they're part of a tradition of Black heroism that goes back decades, and that their version of heroism can be about building up rather than tearing down."

Janelle found herself blinking back tears. "Harold, this is... we can't possibly express how much this means."

"You can express it by doing what you said you'd do," he said simply. "By treating these stories with the respect they deserve and helping them reach the people who need them."

Lena placed the folder on the bed beside Harold. "All the legal paperwork is in here. Transfer of ownership, authentication documents, insurance valuations. Harold's attorney helped him prepare everything months ago."

"There's one condition," Harold added, his voice growing weaker again. "The collection stays together. You don't sell individual issues, you don't split it up. These comics tell a collective story about what positive Black representation can look like, and that story only works when they're seen as part of a larger vision."

"Understood," Demetrius said immediately.

"And Ms. Brooks," Harold continued, "I want a copy of your documentary when it's finished. I may not be here to see it, but Lena will, and she'll know whether you captured what these stories really mean."

The reality of his condition hit Janelle like a physical blow. This wasn't just a transfer of ownership—it was a dying man's final act of cultural stewardship.

"I promise," she said, her voice catching slightly. "I'll make sure the world understands what you preserved and why it mattered."

Harold smiled one last time, the expression radiant despite his obvious exhaustion. "Then my work here is done." He looked toward the window, where the late afternoon sun was casting golden light across the room. "Thirty years of collecting, and it's finally found the right home."

Lena moved to help him settle back against his pillows more comfortably. "You need to rest now," she said gently.

"I will," he agreed. "But first..." He looked back at Janelle and Demetrius with eyes that held three decades of dedication. "Take care of those stories. They represent the best of what we can be, not just as Black people, but as human beings with power who choose to use it well."

As Lena showed them toward the door, Janelle felt the weight of what they'd just received—not just a collection of comics, but a responsibility to preserve and share a vision of heroism that the world desperately needed.

"The collection is in storage unit 247 at Memphis Safe Storage on Union Avenue," Lena said quietly as she handed Demetrius a set of keys. "Harold moved it there last month when it became clear he wouldn't be able to care for it much longer. Everything's climate controlled and properly organized."

They walked to the apartment door in subdued silence,

the magnitude of what had just happened settling over them both.

"Will you let us know...?" Janelle began, then stopped, not sure how to finish the question.

"I'll call you," Lena said simply. "Harold would want to know that the collection made it safely to Sweetgum Meadows."

Outside Harold's apartment building, standing in the early evening air beside Demetrius's SUV, Janelle felt overwhelmed by everything that had changed in the space of a few hours. This morning they'd been strangers on a desperate road trip. Now they were partners in preserving something that represented thirty years of hope and vision.

"We actually did it," Demetrius said quietly, looking down at the keys in his hand.

"We did," Janelle agreed. "But now the real work begins."

They climbed into the SUV, both lost in their own thoughts about the responsibility they'd just accepted. As Demetrius started the engine, Janelle realized that somewhere in that hospital room, between Harold's careful curation and their shared understanding of what the comics represented, something had shifted between them too.

They weren't just professional partners anymore. They were co-guardians of a vision that neither of them could preserve alone.

"So," Demetrius said as they pulled away from Harold's building, "I guess we need to find a hotel for the night and figure out how to get three hundred comics safely back to Sweetgum Meadows."

Janelle nodded, but her mind was already racing ahead to the documentary she would create, the story she would tell about Harold's collection and what it represented. For the first time in months, she felt like she was working on something that mattered more than her career, more than sponsors or network deals.

She was working on something that could change how people understood heroism itself.

And she wasn't doing it alone.

CHAPTER EIGHT

The Memphis Safe Storage facility was exactly what Demetrius had expected—a long, low building with roll-up doors stretching in neat rows, the kind of place where people stored the overflow of their lives. But as he used Harold's key to open unit 247, he wasn't prepared for the careful organization that greeted them.

The comics weren't just stacked in boxes. Harold had created a cataloging system that would have impressed any librarian. Clear plastic storage containers lined metal shelving units, each container labeled with date ranges and themes. "Urban Heroes 1989-1995." "Community Builders 1996-2001." "Family Stories 2002-2007." A small desk in the corner held manila folders filled with what looked like research notes, photocopied interviews, and correspondence with creators.

"He built a research library," Janelle said softly, running her fingers along the labeled containers. "This isn't just collecting. This is scholarship."

The storage unit was climate-controlled, maintaining the

perfect temperature and humidity for preserving paper and ink. Demetrius could see why Harold had moved the collection here—this was better preservation than most people's homes could provide.

"Look at this," Janelle said, opening one of the manila folders on the desk. "Harold corresponded with creators, tracked down original artists, documented publication histories that aren't recorded anywhere else. Some of these comics probably don't exist in any other collection."

Demetrius opened one of the containers and carefully removed a comic he hadn't seen during Harold's presentation. The cover showed a Black teenage girl sitting in what looked like a community garden, her hands glowing as she tended to plants while neighborhood kids watched in fascination. The art style was beautiful, detailed but warm, and the girl's expression was one of calm concentration rather than dramatic heroism.

"*Growing Together* from 1998," he read from the label. "Part of the 'Community Builders' series."

They spent the next two hours in the storage unit, carefully examining sections of the collection. Each container they opened revealed new treasures—comics that reinforced Harold's vision of constructive Black heroism, stories that imagined power used for building rather than destroying.

"We can't take these tonight," Demetrius said finally, reluctantly closing a container of comics from the early 2000s. "Not safely. They need to stay in climate-controlled storage until we can transport them properly."

"You're right," Janelle agreed, though he could see her reluctance to leave the collection behind. "We'll need a proper moving truck tomorrow, something with climate control for the drive back."

They secured the unit and drove through Memphis looking for hotel accommodations. The sun was setting, casting long shadows across the city as they searched for a place to spend the night.

"We did it," Janelle said quietly as they stopped at a red light. "We actually convinced Harold to trust us with thirty years of his life's work."

"We did," Demetrius agreed, though the weight of that responsibility was settling over him. "But now the real work begins."

The first hotel they tried was full. So was the second. The third, a mid-range chain hotel near the interstate, had availability but delivered news that made them both pause.

"We have one room left," the desk clerk said apologetically. "King bed, non-smoking. There's a big convention in town this weekend, and most places are booked solid."

Demetrius glanced at Janelle, who had gone very still beside him. The practical part of his mind noted that they both needed sleep, that they had an early morning ahead of them arranging transport for the collection, and that finding another hotel might mean driving all over Memphis.

The other part of his mind was acutely aware that sharing a hotel room with Janelle would cross a line from professional partnership into something more personal, and he wasn't sure either of them was ready for that complexity.

"We can keep looking," he said quietly. "Try some of the smaller motels further out."

"At this hour? With how tired we both are?" Janelle's voice was carefully controlled, but he caught the slight tension in it. "We need to get some sleep so we can think clearly tomorrow about how to transport the collection safely. We can handle sharing a room for one night."

Her tone was practical, matter-of-fact, but she avoided meeting his eyes as she said it.

"One room, then," he told the clerk, handing over his credit card.

Their room was on the third floor, clean and comfortable with a view of the parking lot. The king-size bed dominated the space, and suddenly it seemed enormous and intimate all at once. There was also a small seating area with a chair and ottoman near the window.

"I can take the chair," Demetrius said immediately, setting his overnight bag on the floor beside it.

"Don't be ridiculous. You're driving eight hours tomorrow, and you're about six feet tall." Janelle dropped her camera bag on the dresser, but her movements were more careful than usual. "The bed is huge. We're both adults."

The matter-of-fact way she said it somehow made the situation feel both more and less complicated. They were adults. They could share sleeping space without it meaning anything beyond the practical necessity of the situation.

But as she moved around the room, checking the curtains and testing the air conditioning, Demetrius found himself noticing things he'd been too focused on business to observe before. The graceful way she moved, how her hair caught the light from the bedside lamp, the unconscious confidence in her gestures even when she was clearly as aware of the intimate setting as he was.

"I'm going to grab some ice and call Mrs. Zhang," he said, needing a few minutes to collect himself. "Let her know we'll be back tomorrow evening."

When he returned with ice from the machine down the hall, Janelle was sitting cross-legged on the bed with her notebook open, sketching what looked like a rough outline for her documentary. She'd changed from her professional clothes into jeans and a soft sweater that made her look younger, more approachable, and the casual intimacy of seeing her in comfortable clothes in a shared bedroom made his chest tighten in a way he hadn't expected.

"How's the planning going?" he asked, settling into the chair with a bottle of water, trying to maintain some physical distance in the small space.

"I keep thinking about what Harold said—that these aren't power fantasies, they're responsibility fantasies." She looked up from her notes, and their eyes met across the small space between the bed and chair. "That's the story I want to tell. Not just about representation, but about what it means when communities imagine their heroes as builders instead of warriors."

There was something in her voice—passion, conviction—that drew him in. He found himself leaning forward slightly, engaged not just in the conversation but in watching her face as she spoke about something that clearly mattered to her deeply.

"It'll be a hard sell to networks," Demetrius said. "They want conflict, drama, clear good guys and bad guys."

"Maybe that's the point." Janelle set her notebook aside and shifted position on the bed, tucking her feet under her. The movement was unselfconscious but somehow intimate in the quiet room. "Maybe the story needs to be told because it's not what networks want. Harold spent thirty years preserving stories that didn't fit the market's idea of what superhero comics should be. Maybe I need to make a documentary that doesn't fit the market's idea of what cultural documentaries should be."

"What will you do if the networks don't pick it up?" he

asked, genuinely curious about this woman who had driven eight hours on the strength of a phone call from a stranger.

"Find another way to tell it. Independent distribution, film festival circuit, streaming platforms." She smiled, and he realized he was memorizing the way her face transformed when she talked about her work. "Harold didn't give up when mainstream publishers weren't interested in his kind of heroes. I won't give up when mainstream media isn't interested in his kind of story."

They talked for another hour, but the conversation had taken on a different quality. In the intimate space of the hotel room, with the day's professional urgency behind them, Demetrius found himself paying attention to things that had nothing to do with comics or documentaries. The way Janelle gestured when she was making a point. How she absently twisted a strand of hair when she was thinking. The occasional moment when their conversation would pause and he'd catch her looking at him with an expression he couldn't quite read.

"I should let you get some sleep," Janelle said finally, glancing at the clock. "Tomorrow's going to be a long day."

The transition to preparing for bed in shared space was more awkward than he had anticipated. They took turns in the bathroom, moving around each other with careful polite-ness in the small room. When Demetrius emerged in his pajama pants and t-shirt, he found Janelle already settled on the far side of the king bed, wearing soft pajamas and looking determinedly focused on her phone.

He settled on the near side of the bed, acutely aware of the space between them and the fact that they were sharing sleeping space like couples did, even though they barely knew each other.

"Good night," Janelle said quietly, reaching to turn off her bedside lamp.

"Good night," he replied, doing the same.

The room fell into darkness, but Demetrius found himself wide awake, hyperaware of every sound—Janelle's breathing gradually evening out, the rustle of sheets when she shifted position, the subtle warmth radiating from her side of the bed.

He lay still, staring at the ceiling and thinking about the day's events. Twelve hours ago, they'd been strangers united only by desperation and opportunity. Now they were lying in the dark together, partners in something that felt far more significant than either of their individual needs.

Somewhere in the quiet darkness, he heard Janelle's breathing change, becoming deeper and more even. He turned his head slightly and could just make out her silhouette in the dim light from the parking lot filtering through the curtains. She'd turned toward him in her sleep, one hand resting on the pillow near the invisible line between their sides of the bed.

The sight made something shift in his chest—an awareness he wasn't quite ready to examine. When had he started noticing the way she looked when she wasn't performing the role of documentary filmmaker? When had he started caring whether she was comfortable in his presence?

The questions unsettled him. He'd spent eight years building careful boundaries around his personal life, and now this woman he'd known for less than a day had somehow slipped past his defenses simply by being present, by caring about the same things he cared about, by looking peaceful in sleep beside him.

As he finally drifted toward sleep, Demetrius tried not to

think about what tomorrow would bring—not just the logistics of moving Harold's collection, but the reality of spending another eight hours in close quarters with someone who was making him question assumptions he'd held about himself for nearly a decade.

CHAPTER NINE

Janelle woke to the sound of Demetrius's voice, low and careful as he spoke on the phone, and for a moment, she forgot where she was. Hotel room. Memphis. Harold's collection. The memories came flooding back as she opened her eyes to find sunlight streaming through the curtains and Demetrius already dressed, sitting in the chair by the window.

"Yes, ma'am, climate-controlled transport," he was saying quietly. "Three hundred twelve individually sleeved comics, plus research materials. We need them to arrive in the same condition they're stored."

She lay still for a moment, watching him handle the logistics with the same careful attention he'd shown Harold's comics. There was something reassuring about his methodical approach, the way he asked specific questions about temperature control and padding materials. This wasn't just business for him—it was stewardship of something precious.

When he ended the call, she sat up, suddenly aware that her hair was probably a mess and she was still wearing pajamas while he was fully dressed and handling important arrangements.

"Good morning," she said, pushing her hair back from her face. "Any luck with the transport?"

"Morning." His smile was a little awkward, and she realized this was as strange for him as it was for her—waking up in shared space with someone he barely knew. "I found a company that specializes in art and collectibles transport. They can have a climate-controlled truck here by noon."

"That's perfect." She swung her legs out of bed, then paused, acutely aware that getting ready in shared space would require some coordination. "I'll just..."

"I'll grab coffee from the lobby," Demetrius said quickly, seeming to understand her hesitation. "Give you some time to get ready."

After he left, Janelle stood in the middle of the hotel room, struck by how intimate the space felt with evidence of both of them scattered around—his overnight bag, her camera equipment, the impression of where they'd both slept in the large bed. Last night had been more charged than she'd expected, lying in the dark aware of his presence just a few feet away, listening to the sound of his breathing and wondering what she was doing sharing a bed with a man she'd met yesterday.

But it hadn't felt wrong. That was what unsettled her. Despite the circumstances that had brought them together, despite knowing him for less than twenty-four hours, sleeping beside Demetrius had felt surprisingly natural. Safe, even.

She shook her head and focused on getting ready. They had work to do.

By the time Demetrius returned with coffee and pastries

from the hotel lobby, she was dressed and had her equipment packed.

"The transport company wants to meet us at the storage facility at noon," he said, handing her a coffee cup. "We can supervise the loading and follow them back to Sweetgum Meadows. Should put us home by early evening."

"Home," Janelle repeated, testing the word. She'd been living out of her van for months, documenting other people's homes and communities. The idea of having a destination that felt like home was foreign.

"I mean, back to Sweetgum Meadows," Demetrius corrected quickly, and she caught the slight awkwardness in his tone. "You'll probably want to find somewhere to stay while you're working on the documentary."

"Right," she agreed, though something in her chest tightened at the reminder that she was still essentially homeless. "I'm thinking this will take several weeks to document properly. I'll need to film the collection's arrival, interview you about your plans for integrating it into the store, and follow some of the young people as they discover it."

"Jerome would probably be willing to be interviewed," Demetrius said. "That little girl too, if her grandmother agrees. And there are others—teenagers who've been looking for heroes who look like them, kids who love stories but haven't found the right ones yet."

As they talked through the logistics, Janelle found herself studying Demetrius's face, noting how animated he became when discussing the potential impact on his community. This wasn't just about running a business for him. It was about changing lives, one comic book at a time.

"What made you choose comics?" she asked. "I mean, you

could serve your community in lots of ways. Why a comic book store specifically?"

Demetrius was quiet for a moment, and she thought he might deflect the question. Then he set down his coffee cup and looked directly at her.

"When I was eight years old, my grandfather took me to a comic book store in Atlanta," he said. "First time I'd ever been in one. I was looking through the superhero comics, and I kept flipping past all these characters who didn't look like me, didn't live in places that felt familiar, didn't deal with problems that seemed real to my experience."

He paused, and she could see the memory playing out in his mind.

"My grandfather noticed what I was doing and asked the store owner if there were any comics with Black heroes. The guy looked at us like we'd asked for something impossible. Said there wasn't much call for that kind of thing." Demetrius's expression darkened slightly. "My grandfather bought me three comics anyway—all featuring Black characters, all from small publishers I'd never heard of."

"What were they?"

"One was about a teenage boy in Detroit who could talk to animals and used his power to help his neighbors solve problems. Another featured a Black woman who was a doctor by day and fought injustice by night, but not with violence—with evidence and organization. The third was about a group of kids from different backgrounds who worked together to clean up their neighborhood."

Janelle felt her documentary instincts engaging. "Those sound like the kinds of stories Harold was preserving."

"They were exactly the kinds of stories Harold was preserving. And they changed everything for me." Demetrius leaned forward, his voice gaining intensity. "For the first time, I saw heroes who looked like me, who cared about the things I cared about, who used their powers to build things up instead of tear them down. I went back to that store every week for two years, hunting for more stories like those."

"Did you find them?"

"Some. Not many. Most of those small publishers went out of business, and the mainstream companies were just starting to experiment with Black characters who weren't stereotypes." He shrugged. "But I found enough to know that these stories existed, and that they mattered. When I opened Nerd Central, I made sure it would be the kind of place my grandfather and I should have found that first day—a place where every kid could find heroes who looked like them."

Janelle set down her coffee, struck by the parallel between Demetrius's story and Harold's mission. "Harold spent thirty years preserving exactly the kinds of stories that changed your life."

"I know," Demetrius said softly. "That's why yesterday felt like... like everything coming full circle. Harold saved the stories that mainstream comic stores couldn't keep alive."

She found herself leaning forward, drawn into the conversation and the passion behind it. "And now you get to share them with kids who are looking for the same thing you were looking for."

"Right. Jerome, that little girl, all the others—they won't have to settle for whatever's available. They'll have access to thirty years' worth of heroes who show them that power can be used constructively, that heroism can look like community building and healing and education."

The way he talked about the kids who came into his store, the care in his voice when he discussed their needs and dreams, made something warm spread through Janelle's chest. This wasn't abstract community service for him. These were relationships, individual young people whose lives he was genuinely invested in changing.

"You really love them," she observed. "The kids who come into your store."

Demetrius looked surprised by the comment, then thoughtful. "I guess I do. They remind me of myself at that age, looking for stories that told me I could be heroic too. If I can help them find those stories earlier than I did, maybe they'll spend less time doubting their own potential."

The conversation was interrupted by his phone ringing. The transport company, confirming details for the pickup.

As they gathered their things and prepared to check out of the hotel, Janelle found herself thinking about the story she wanted to tell. It wasn't just about Harold's collection or even about representation in comics. It was about the ripple effects of cultural preservation—how one person's thirty-year mission to save stories could transform a comic book store, which could transform a community, which could transform individual lives.

And it was about people like Demetrius, who understood that serving a community meant more than selling products. It meant creating spaces where young people could find the stories they needed to imagine better versions of themselves.

"Ready?" Demetrius asked, shouldering his overnight bag.

"Ready," she confirmed, though as they walked toward the elevator, she realized she wasn't just ready for the logistics of transporting Harold's collection. She was ready to document something that mattered, to tell a story that could change how people understood the power of representation and community investment.

She was ready to spend the next several weeks in Sweetgum Meadows, working alongside a man who was making her question everything she thought she knew about belonging, about home, about the difference between documenting community and actually being part of one.

The elevator doors closed behind them, and Janelle caught their reflection in the polished metal—two people who'd shared a hotel room and morning coffee, who were about to drive eight hours together with a collection of irreplaceable comics, who had somehow become partners in something that felt much more significant than either of them had planned.

The thought both thrilled and terrified her.

CHAPTER TEN

The climate-controlled transport truck was everything Demetrius had hoped for—professional, careful, equipped with the kind of padding and temperature controls that would keep Harold's collection safe during the eight-hour journey back to Georgia. He and Janelle supervised every step of the loading process, watching as the transport crew carefully moved each container from the storage unit to the truck with the reverence the comics deserved.

"Thirty years of collecting," Janelle murmured as they watched the final container disappear into the truck. "And now it's really happening."

"Harold would be proud," Demetrius said, though he wondered how the dying man was doing today. Yesterday felt like a lifetime ago, but it had been less than twenty-four hours since they'd sat beside his bed and proven themselves worthy of his life's work.

The drive back to Sweetgum Meadows started comfortably enough. They followed the transport truck at a careful distance, both of them occasionally checking to make sure the precious cargo was still secure. The conversation flowed naturally—more stories about Harold's collection, plans for integrating the comics into Nerd Central, ideas for Janelle's documentary.

But somewhere around the Tennessee-Georgia border, the comfortable partnership dynamic began to shift into something more complex.

"Can I ask you something?" Janelle said during a stretch of highway where the transport truck was easily visible ahead of them.

"Sure."

"Yesterday, when Harold was showing us those comics, there was a moment when you looked at me and I could see something register for you. Like you understood something about me that you hadn't before." She paused. "What was it?"

The directness of the question caught him off guard. He thought back to Harold's presentation, remembering the moment she'd described authentic cultural preservation versus exploitation, the conviction in her voice when she'd talked about serving communities rather than marketing to outsiders.

"You weren't just giving Harold the answers you thought he wanted to hear," Demetrius said slowly. "You actually understood what he was trying to preserve, and why it mattered. A lot of people would have focused on the monetary value or the historical significance, but you saw the human impact."

"And that surprised you?"

"It did," he admitted. "I've met a lot of people who talk about cultural preservation, but most of them are more interested in the preservation than the culture. You're interested in the people who need these stories."

Janelle was quiet for a moment, and he wondered if he'd said something wrong. Then she spoke, her voice softer than usual.

"I've spent five years documenting communities I could never really be part of. Always the outsider with the camera, always leaving before I got too attached." She stared out the passenger window at the Georgia countryside rolling past. "But yesterday, listening to Harold talk about those comics, sitting in that room with you... it was the first time I felt like I wasn't just documenting something. I was part of it."

The admission hung in the air between them, and Demetrius felt that familiar awareness he'd been trying to ignore since they'd shared the hotel room.

"Is that what you want?" he asked. "To be part of something instead of just documenting it?"

"I don't know," Janelle said honestly. "It scares me. Being part of something means you can lose it. You can disappoint people, or they can decide you don't belong after all."

"Or you can belong somewhere long enough to make it better."

She turned to look at him, and he caught the vulnerability in her expression before she looked away again. "I don't have a great track record with belonging."

They drove in silence for several miles after that, the weight of the conversation settling between them. Demetrius found himself thinking about his own relationship with belonging—how he'd chosen Sweetgum Meadows over his ex-wife's demands to leave, how he'd built his life around serving a community rather than risking intimate relationships.

"What about you?" Janelle asked eventually. "You've built this whole life around helping other people belong, but do you ever feel like you're holding yourself apart from the community you serve?"

The question was uncomfortably perceptive. "What do you mean?"

"I mean, you know everyone in town, you serve their kids, you're obviously respected and valued. But you live alone, you work alone, and from what I've seen, you're very careful about maintaining professional boundaries with everyone."

"That's not true," he protested, though even as he said it, he realized she might have a point.

"When was the last time you had dinner with someone that wasn't business-related? When was the last time you let someone take care of you instead of you taking care of them?"

The questions made him uncomfortable because he couldn't readily answer them. Mrs. Zhang brought him food, but that was neighborly commerce. The kids came to his store, but he was their mentor, not their peer. His sister called from Atlanta, but their conversations were mostly about her family's needs.

"I serve my community," he said finally. "That's enough."

"Is it?" Janelle's voice was gentle, not challenging. "Because from where I'm sitting, it looks like you've created a life where you're indispensable to everyone but not particularly close to anyone."

The observation stung because it felt true. After Denise had left, after he'd chosen the community over their relationship, he'd gradually built walls around his personal life. Not obvious walls—he was friendly, helpful, available. But walls nonetheless.

"Maybe that's safer," he said quietly.

"Maybe it is. But maybe it's also lonely."

They were approaching a rest area, and Demetrius found himself needing a break from the intensity of the conversation. "Want to stop? Check on the truck driver, stretch our legs?"

"Sure."

The rest area was busy with afternoon travelers, families corralling tired children and truckers stretching their legs. The transport driver assured them that everything was secure and climate-controlled, the comics riding safely in their controlled environment.

As they walked back toward Demetrius's SUV, Janelle stopped suddenly and pulled out her camera.

"What are you filming?" he asked.

"You," she said, raising the camera. "Talk to me about Harold's collection. What it means to you, what you hope it will mean to your community."

"Janelle, I don't think—"

"Please. Just for a minute. I want to capture this moment, the anticipation before the collection arrives in Sweetgum Meadows."

He looked at the camera, then at her face behind it, and realized this was the first time since they'd met that she was fully in her professional role while he was being asked to be vulnerable. The dynamic felt different, more formal, and he wasn't sure he was ready for it.

"I'm not good at being interviewed," he said.

"You don't have to be good at it. Just be honest." Her voice was gentle but persistent. "Tell me what yesterday meant to you."

Demetrius glanced around the rest area, aware of other travelers moving past them, then back at Janelle's expectant face. Something in her expression—not just professional interest, but genuine curiosity about his thoughts—made him decide to trust her with his honesty.

"Harold's collection represents thirty years of someone believing that stories matter," he said slowly. "Not just any stories, but stories that show Black characters as builders, healers, problem-solvers. Stories that imagine what we could be when we're not defined by trauma or reaction to oppression."

He paused, finding his rhythm as the words came easier.

"When I was a kid, I had to hunt for heroes who looked like me. Most of the time, I settled for whatever was available, or I just imagined that the white characters were somehow like me." He looked directly at the camera. "The kids who come into my store—Jerome, that little girl with her grandmother, all the others—they won't have to settle. They'll have access to decades' worth of heroes who show them that power can be used to build communities, to heal wounds, to solve problems without violence."

"And what do you hope that will change?"

"Everything," Demetrius said simply. "When kids see themselves reflected in heroic narratives from an early age, they start imagining themselves as capable of heroic things. Not just surviving their circumstances, but transforming them."

Janelle lowered the camera, and he saw something in her expression that looked like admiration mixed with something deeper.

"That was perfect," she said quietly.

The moment stretched between them, professional boundaries blurring into something more personal. Demetrius found himself studying her face, noting the way she looked at him when she wasn't hiding behind the camera's lens.

"We should get back on the road," he said finally, though he made no move toward the SUV.

"Yeah," she agreed, though she didn't move either.

They stood there in the parking lot of a highway rest area, Harold's collection in the truck ahead of them, eight years of careful emotional distance suddenly feeling like something Demetrius might be willing to risk closing.

The sound of a car horn broke the spell, and they both stepped back, the professional dynamic reasserting itself.

"The truck's moving," Janelle observed, nodding toward the transport vehicle that was indeed pulling back onto the highway.

"Right. We should follow."

As they got back into the SUV and merged onto the interstate, Demetrius found himself thinking about the interview, about the way Janelle had looked at him when he'd spoken about transforming circumstances rather than just surviving them.

"Can I ask you something now?" he said as they settled into the rhythm of following the transport truck.

"Sure."

"When you document other communities, do you ever want to stay? To become part of what you're filming instead of just observing it?"

Janelle was quiet for a long moment. "Sometimes," she

said finally. "But wanting something and believing you deserve it are different things."

"What do you mean?"

"I mean that I've spent most of my life as a temporary resident in other people's homes. I know how to be grateful, how to be helpful, how to not be a burden. But I don't know how to believe that someone might actually want me to stay permanently."

The vulnerability in her admission made something ache in Demetrius's chest. "What if someone did want you to stay?"

"I don't know," she said honestly. "I think I'd probably find a way to convince myself they were just being polite."

They drove in silence for several miles after that, both of them processing the conversation and its implications. The transport truck maintained its steady pace ahead of them, carrying Harold's thirty years of preserved hope toward a community that didn't yet know how much their understanding of heroism was about to expand.

"We're really doing this," Janelle said eventually, watching the truck ahead of them.

"We really are," Demetrius agreed.

"Are you nervous?"

"Terrified," he admitted. "This collection is going to change everything about how I run the store, how I serve the community. And I'm doing it in partnership with someone I met two days ago."

"Technically, it was yesterday."

"That makes it worse, not better."

Janelle laughed, and the sound filled the SUV with something lighter than the serious conversations they'd been having. "Well, when you put it like that, this does seem like a terrible idea."

"The worst," Demetrius agreed, but he was smiling too.

"But we're doing it anyway."

"We're doing it anyway."

The late afternoon sun was beginning to cast long shadows across the highway as they crossed into Georgia, Harold's collection riding safely ahead of them toward its new home in Sweetgum Meadows. In a few hours, they would arrive at a community that had sent out two strangers yesterday morning and was about to receive back two people who had somehow become partners in something that felt much larger than either of them had planned.

Demetrius glanced at Janelle, who was making notes in her ever-present notebook, already planning how to document the collection's arrival and impact. Tomorrow, she would begin filming the story of how Harold's thirty-year mission continued its work of transformation.

Tomorrow would bring new challenges, new questions about how to integrate the collection into his store, how to serve his community with this expanded vision of heroism. And somewhere in all of that work, he would need to figure out what this partnership with Janelle actually meant, and whether the connection he felt growing between them was something worth exploring or just the intensity of shared purpose.

For now, though, it was enough to drive toward home with Harold's collection safely ahead of them, knowing that whatever came next, they would face it together.

CHAPTER ELEVEN

The first thing Janelle noticed when they arrived in Sweetgum Meadows was the crowd gathered outside Nerd Central Comics. Word had apparently traveled through the small town about the collection's arrival, and what looked like half the community had come out to witness the moment.

Mrs. Zhang stood near the front of the group, talking animatedly with Rochelle Stevens, who had apparently left the bed and breakfast in Benjamin's capable hands to witness the collection's arrival. Several teenagers clustered together on the sidewalk, including Jerome, who was practically bouncing on his toes with excitement. Mrs. Washington, the elderly woman whose biscuit recipe had been Janelle's first interview in Sweetgum Meadows, was organizing what looked like a welcoming committee of neighbors carrying folding chairs and coolers.

"I should have expected this," Demetrius said, pulling his SUV up behind the transport truck. "News travels fast in a town this size."

"Do you mind the audience?" Janelle asked, already reaching for her camera bag. This was exactly the kind of authentic community response she'd hoped to document.

"No," Demetrius said, though she caught a note of nervousness in his voice. "These people have been waiting for something like this for years. They deserve to be part of it."

The transport crew was already lowering the truck's lift gate when Demetrius and Janelle approached. The crowd pressed closer, everyone trying to get a glimpse of the climate-controlled containers that held Harold's thirty years of collecting.

"Mr. D!" Jerome called out, pushing through the gathering. "Is it true? Did you really get the Black Heroes collection?"

"We did," Demetrius confirmed, and a cheer went up from the assembled group.

Janelle raised her camera, filming the spontaneous celebration, the joy on faces young and old as the first container was carefully wheeled from the truck into the comic store. This was what she'd been hoping to capture—genuine community excitement about cultural preservation, people understanding instinctively that they were witnessing something significant.

Mrs. Zhang appeared at her elbow. "You must be the documentary filmmaker. I'm Mei Zhang. Welcome to Sweetgum Meadows."

"Janelle Brooks. Thank you for the warm welcome."

"Demetrius called yesterday to tell me about your success with Mr. Murphy. The whole town has been talking about it." Mrs. Zhang's eyes were bright with curiosity and approval. "You'll be staying to film the collection's impact?"

"That's the plan," Janelle said, then hesitated. "Though I haven't arranged accommodations yet."

"The bed and breakfast is lovely, and Benjamin and Rochelle are very reasonable for long-term guests. If you're staying for several weeks, I'm sure they'd offer you the extended-stay rate."

The practical reminder made Janelle's stomach tighten slightly. Extended-stay rates were still rates, and her financial situation hadn't magically improved just because she'd helped secure Harold's collection. But she pushed the worry aside—she'd figure out the logistics later.

The transport crew worked methodically, moving each container with careful precision while the crowd watched in fascination. Janelle filmed it all: Demetrius directing the placement of containers in his store's back room, children pressing their faces to the front windows trying to see inside, elderly residents sharing stories about the comics they'd read as children.

"Ms. Brooks?" A young voice interrupted her filming.

She lowered the camera to find a girl of about nine standing beside her, the same child she'd seen through the store window on her first day in town.

"I'm Tia," the girl said shyly. "Mr. D says you're making a movie about the new comics."

"I am," Janelle confirmed, crouching down to the girl's eye level. "Are you excited about the collection?"

"Yes, ma'am. Mr. D told my uncle Sean that there are stories about girls who look like me who have superpowers and use them to help people." Tia's eyes were bright with anticipation. "I've been writing my own stories, but I want to see what real authors wrote."

"What kind of stories do you write?"

"Stories about a girl who can talk to plants and helps her neighborhood grow a community garden," Tia said matter-of-factly. "And sometimes she helps solve problems between neighbors by getting the flowers to tell her what really happened."

Janelle felt her heart squeeze. "That sounds like exactly the kind of story that's in Mr. Murphy's collection."

"Really?" Tia's face lit up.

"Really. Would you be willing to let me film you reading some of the new comics? I'd love to document how young writers like you respond to these stories."

"Can I ask my uncle Sean first?"

"Of course."

As Tia ran off to find her uncle, Janelle realized she'd just had her first real interaction with someone in Sweetgum Meadows that wasn't mediated through Demetrius or professional necessity. Tia had approached her as a community member, someone who belonged here enough to be trusted with excitement and dreams.

The feeling was unsettling and wonderful at the same time.

"Getting your first taste of Sweetgum Meadows hospitality?" Demetrius appeared beside her, looking slightly overwhelmed but pleased by the community turnout.

"Tia is amazing," Janelle said. "She's already writing stories that sound like they came from Harold's collection."

"She's one of our brightest. Her uncle Sean and aunt Nevaeh have done a wonderful job raising her, and the whole family is creative. She's been asking about the collection ever since I mentioned it to Nevaeh."

The final container was wheeled into the store, and the transport crew began packing up their equipment. The crowd started to disperse, but several people lingered, clearly hoping for a preview of the collection.

Mrs. Washington approached them with a warm smile. "Mr. Lakeson, Ms. Brooks, would you consider joining us for dinner tonight? Nothing fancy, just a community meal to celebrate the collection's arrival. Rochelle and I thought it would be a nice welcome for Ms. Brooks and a proper celebration for you both."

Janelle glanced at Demetrius, unsure what the protocol was for accepting community invitations when she was technically there to document rather than participate.

"That's very kind," Demetrius said. "But we're both pretty tired from the drive, and I need to start organizing the collection."

"The collection will still be there tomorrow," Mrs. Washington said firmly. "Tonight is for celebrating what you've accomplished. Six o'clock at Rochelle's Diner. The whole community is invited."

It wasn't really a request, Janelle realized. It was a gentle command from someone accustomed to organizing community events.

"We'll be there," she heard herself saying. "Thank you for including me."

As Mrs. Washington walked away, looking satisfied, Demetrius turned to Janelle with a slightly amused expression.

"You just accepted a dinner invitation to a community celebration in your honor," he said. "You realize that means you're officially part of this now, not just documenting it?"

The observation made her stomach flutter with something between excitement and panic. "Is that a problem?"

"No," Demetrius said, and something in his tone made her

look at him more carefully. "I think it's exactly what Harold would have wanted. His collection was never meant to sit in isolation. It was meant to bring people together."

That evening, as Janelle sat in Rochelle's Old-Fashioned Diner surrounded by the warm chatter of community members celebrating Harold's collection, she found herself thinking about belonging in ways she never had before. She wasn't just documenting Sweetgum Meadows—she was experiencing it. She wasn't just observing how the collection would impact the community—she was part of that impact.

Jerome sat across from her, describing the comics he most wanted to read. Tia had convinced Sean to let her participate in the documentary and was already planning which stories she'd share on camera. Mrs. Zhang kept refilling her sweet tea and asking thoughtful questions about her previous documentary work.

And Demetrius sat beside her, occasionally catching her eye with expressions she couldn't quite interpret, as if he was seeing her differently in this community context.

"So what's next?" Rochelle asked during a lull in the conversation. "When do we get to see these famous comics?"

"Tomorrow," Demetrius promised. "I need to organize them properly first, make sure they're displayed in a way that honors Harold's vision. But by this weekend, they'll be available for the community to explore."

"And Ms. Brooks will be filming our reactions," Jerome added excitedly. "We're going to be in a real documentary."

"That's right," Janelle confirmed, though as she looked around the table at the eager faces, she realized her documentary was evolving into something different than she'd originally planned. This wasn't just about Harold's collection or representation in comics. It was about what happened when a community gained access to stories that reflected their highest aspirations rather than their survival struggles.

As the evening wound down and people began to head home, Janelle found herself reluctant to leave the warm atmosphere of the diner. This was what she'd been documenting for years without experiencing—the sense of being part of something larger than herself, of belonging somewhere that valued her contribution.

"Need a ride back to the bed and breakfast?" Demetrius asked as they stood outside the diner.

"Actually, I should probably find Benjamin or Rochelle and arrange for a room," Janelle said, reality reasserting itself. "I haven't actually booked anything yet."

"Janelle." Demetrius's voice was quiet but firm. "You told me you have thirty dollars to your name. You can't afford weeks at the bed and breakfast, even with an extended-stay rate."

Heat rose in her cheeks. She'd forgotten that she'd been so honest with him during their desperate partnership negotiations. "I'll figure something out. Maybe I can work out a payment plan, or—"

"There's an apartment above my store," he interrupted. "Two bedrooms, fully furnished. No one's using it right now since I have my own house."

The offer caught her completely off guard. "Demetrius, I can't—"

"You can, and you should. You'll be documenting the community's response to the collection. It makes sense for you to be right there where the action is happening." He paused, looking slightly uncomfortable with his own generosity. "Besides, Harold wanted his collection to bring people together. Having you live above where it's housed seems fitting."

"I don't know what to say."

"Say yes. It's practical for everyone involved."

The matter-of-fact way he presented it made it feel less like charity and more like a sensible business arrangement. But standing there in the warm evening air, looking at this man who barely knew her but was willing to solve her housing crisis without making her feel like a burden, Janelle felt something shift in her chest.

"Yes," she said quietly. "Thank you. I'll pay you back when—"

"We'll worry about that later," he said. "Right now, let's get you settled so you can focus on telling Harold's story."

As they walked back toward his SUV, Janelle realized that once again, Demetrius had found a way to take care of her practical needs while making it about the mission they shared rather than her personal circumstances.

Tomorrow would be a big day—the first day of documenting how Harold's collection transformed a community. And she'd be living right above the comics that had brought them together, in a space offered by a man who was making her question everything she thought she knew about belonging, about trust, and about the difference between documenting community and actually being part of one.

CHAPTER TWELVE

The apartment above Nerd Central hadn't been occupied in three years, not since the previous tenant had moved to Atlanta for a job. Demetrius had kept it clean and maintained, occasionally using it for storage or as a quiet retreat when the store got busy, but he'd never seriously considered renting it out again. As he unlocked the door and flipped on the lights, he tried to see the space through Janelle's eyes.

Two bedrooms, a small but functional kitchen, a living area with windows that overlooked Main Street. The furniture was simple but comfortable—a couch and coffee table he'd bought when he first opened the store, a dining table that had belonged to his grandmother, a bed in the master bedroom that he'd never actually slept in. It was clean, furnished, and completely impersonal.

"This is perfect," Janelle said behind him, and he heard genuine relief in her voice. She set her camera bag down carefully and looked around the space with the assessing eye of someone who'd learned to make the best of temporary accommodations. "Are you sure about this? I don't want to impose."

"You're not imposing. Like I said, no one's using it." He gestured toward the kitchen. "Everything works—refrigerator, stove, coffee maker. Internet password is on that note by the router. The shower has good water pressure."

The practical details felt safer than acknowledging the real reason he'd offered her the apartment: the thought of her sleeping in her van for weeks while documenting Harold's collection had made something twist uncomfortably in his chest. She'd driven eight hours on the strength of a stranger's phone call, convinced a dying man to trust her with his life's work, and was now committed to telling a story that mattered more than profit or recognition. The least he could do was make sure she had a decent place to sleep.

"The washer and dryer are in the closet off the kitchen," he continued, moving toward the windows to check that they opened properly. "And you're right above the store, so you'll be able to hear if anyone's breaking in to steal Harold's collection."

Janelle smiled at that. "Very practical security arrangement."

"That's me. Practical." But even as he said it, he knew offering the apartment wasn't entirely practical. It was generous in a way that made him vulnerable, that suggested he cared about her comfort and wellbeing beyond their professional partnership.

"Demetrius." Her voice was quieter now, and when he turned, she was looking at him with an expression he couldn't quite read. "Thank you. Not just for the apartment, but for... all of it. The partnership, trusting me with Harold's test, bringing me into the community. I know you didn't have to do any of that."

"Harold chose both of us," he said. "I just provided transportation."

"You provided a lot more than transportation." She walked to the front windows and looked down at Main Street, where the evening was settling over Sweetgum Meadows with the peaceful quiet of a small town winding down. "You made it possible for me to be part of something instead of just documenting it."

The admission hung between them, and Demetrius found himself studying her profile as she gazed out the window. There was something different about her expression when she thought no one was watching—less of the professional competence she wore like armor, more of the vulnerability she'd shown during their drive back from Memphis.

"Are you nervous?" he asked. "About tomorrow, I mean. Starting the real documentation work."

"Terrified," she admitted without turning around. "This story could change everything for me professionally. But more than that, it matters. These comics, Harold's vision, what it could mean for kids like Tia and Jerome—I want to do it justice."

"You will."

"How can you be so sure?"

"Because you asked the right questions," Demetrius said simply. "When Harold was testing us, you didn't focus on market value or historical significance. You understood that those comics were about showing people what they could become when they weren't defined by trauma or oppression. That's not something you can fake."

Janelle turned from the window, and he caught something in her expression that made his chest tighten in the way that had been happening more frequently since Memphis. "What if I mess this up? What if I can't capture what these stories really mean to the community?"

"Then you'll figure it out and try again," he said. "That's what people do when something matters to them."

The simple confidence in his voice seemed to steady her. She nodded, taking a deep breath and straightening her shoulders in the gesture he was beginning to recognize as her way of preparing for challenges.

"I should let you get settled," Demetrius said, though he found himself reluctant to leave. The apartment felt different with her in it—warmer, more alive. "Tomorrow's going to start early. I want to have the collection organized and properly displayed before the community starts arriving."

"What time do you usually open the store?"

"Ten AM, but I'll be there by seven to work on the setup. You're welcome to come down and film the preparation process if you think it would be useful for the documentary."

"That would be perfect. The story should include how much care goes into presenting Harold's vision properly."

As he moved toward the door, Janelle called his name softly.

"Demetrius?"

He turned back to find her standing in the middle of the living room, looking smaller somehow in the empty space, but determined.

"I meant what I said earlier. About wanting to be part of something instead of just documenting it. I know I'm not great at staying in one place, and I know this whole situation is... complicated. But I want you to know that I'm committed to this. To Harold's story, to the community's response, to doing this right."

"I know you are."

"And I'm grateful. For the partnership, for your trust, for..." She gestured around the apartment. "For giving me a place to belong while I figure out what comes next."

The word 'belong' hung in the air between them, carrying weight that he wasn't ready to examine. Demetrius felt the familiar urge to retreat, to maintain the professional boundaries that had kept him safe for eight years. But looking at Janelle standing in the apartment above his store, surrounded by his furniture and his trust, he realized that those boundaries had already shifted without his permission.

"Good night, Janelle," he said quietly.

"Good night."

He closed the apartment door behind him and stood in the narrow hallway for a moment, listening to the soft sounds of her moving around the space above his store. Tomorrow, she would begin documenting how Harold's collection transformed his community. But tonight, as he walked home to his own house for the first time in years with someone else living above his store, Demetrius realized that the transformation had already begun.

The collection hadn't just brought new stories to Sweetgum Meadows. It had brought Janelle—a woman who was making him question the careful solitude he'd built around his personal life, who was making him wonder whether serving his community might be even more meaningful when shared with someone who understood why it mattered.

As he unlocked his own front door and stepped into the familiar quiet of his house, Demetrius found himself unsettled by how different the evening had felt. For eight years, he'd come home to the same routine, the same solitude, the same careful distance from complications that might disrupt the life he'd built. Tonight, knowing someone was living above his store—someone who understood what Harold's collection meant, who cared about the same things he cared about—made his house feel emptier than it ever had before.

He wasn't sure what that meant, and he wasn't sure he was ready to find out.

But first, they had thirty years of preserved hope to organize and three hundred stories of constructive heroism to share with a community that was ready to see themselves reflected in narratives of possibility rather than survival.

It was going to be a very good day.

CHAPTER THIRTEEN

*J*anelle woke to the sound of movement below her in the comic store, and for a moment, she couldn't remember where she was. Then the events of the previous day came flooding back—Harold's collection, the community celebration, Demetrius offering her the apartment. She checked her phone: 6:47 AM. He'd said he'd be in the store by seven to organize the collection.

She dressed quickly and grabbed her camera, wanting to capture the careful process of presenting Harold's thirty years of curation to the community. This was exactly the kind of behind-the-scenes documentation that would help viewers understand the reverence and responsibility involved in cultural preservation.

When she made her way downstairs through the connecting door Demetrius had shown her the night before, she found him in the store's back room, carefully removing comics from their storage containers and examining each one with the attention of someone handling sacred texts.

"Good morning," she said softly, not wanting to startle him.

"Morning." He looked up from a comic featuring a Black woman in a lab coat whose hands were glowing with some kind of energy. "I hope I didn't wake you."

"Not at all. I wanted to film this part if you don't mind. The preparation process is important to the story."

"Of course." He held up the comic he'd been examining. "*Dr. Synthesis* from 1994. She's a biochemist who can manipulate molecular structures to heal diseases. The art is incredible—look at how they drew her laboratory."

Janelle raised her camera, filming as Demetrius explained the comic's significance, his voice carrying the same passion she'd heard when he talked about the kids who came into his store. This wasn't just inventory organization. This was curatorial work, deciding how to present Harold's vision in a way that would maximize its impact on the community.

"How are you organizing them?" she asked, lowering the camera momentarily.

"By themes, mostly. Harold had them sorted by publication dates and publishers, but I think they'll be more meaningful to readers if they're grouped by the types of heroes and the kinds of problems they solve." He gestured toward several piles he'd created on a large worktable. "Healers, teachers, community builders, problem solvers, family protectors. Each group tells a different story about what Black heroism can look like."

"That's brilliant. You're not just displaying Harold's collection—you're interpreting his philosophy."

Something in Demetrius's expression shifted, and she realized she'd hit on something important. "Exactly. These comics were never meant to be museum pieces. They were meant to be read, discussed, internalized. Harold preserved them so kids could discover that their power—their intelligence, their creativity, their capacity for building community—that these are heroic qualities."

As the morning progressed, Janelle documented the meticulous process of selection and display. Demetrius chose representative comics from each thematic group for prominent display, with the rest organized in accessible bins where community members could browse at their leisure. He created small explanatory cards for each display area, written in language that would appeal to both children and adults.

"This is incredibly thoughtful," Janelle observed, filming him as he adjusted the placement of a comic about a teenage boy whose superpower was enhanced empathy that he used to mediate conflicts in his school. "You're creating an entire educational experience."

"Jerome's going to love that one," Demetrius said, stepping back to assess his work. "He's been dealing with some bullying situations at school. Seeing a hero who uses emotional intelligence to solve problems might give him some new strategies."

The care in his voice when he mentioned Jerome made Janelle's chest tighten with something she wasn't ready to examine. Demetrius wasn't just running a business or even serving his community in an abstract sense. He was thinking about specific young people, about their individual needs and challenges, about how Harold's collection could impact their daily lives.

"Can I ask you something?" she said, setting down her camera for a moment.

"Sure."

"When you decided to open this store fifteen years ago, did you know it would become this? A place where kids come not just to buy comics but to figure out who they want to be?"

Demetrius was quiet for a moment, organizing a display of comics featuring Black families and community networks. "I knew I wanted to create the kind of space I would have loved as a kid. A place where seeing yourself in heroic narratives wasn't rare or special—it was normal. But I didn't anticipate how much it would change me too."

"How has it changed you?"

"It's taught me that serving a community isn't just about providing what people need. It's about helping them discover what's possible." He looked directly at her, and she felt that familiar flutter of recognition. "These kids come in here looking for entertainment, but they leave understanding that they have the power to transform their circumstances, not just survive them."

The bell above the store's front door chimed, and they both turned to see Mrs. Zhang entering with what looked like a breakfast tray.

"I thought you might need sustenance before the community invasion," she said, setting the tray on the front counter. "Coffee, pastries, and some of those breakfast sandwiches you like."

"Mrs. Zhang, you didn't have to—"

"Of course I did. Today is important." She looked around the store, taking in the carefully organized displays of Harold's collection. "This is beautiful work, Demetrius. You can see how much thought you've put into this."

"Thank you." He accepted a coffee cup gratefully. "I hope the community feels the same way."

"They will." Mrs. Zhang turned to Janelle with a warm smile. "And how was your first night above the store? Comfortable?"

"Very comfortable. Demetrius has been incredibly generous." Janelle paused, looking between them with amusement. "Should I even ask how you already know where I'm staying?"

"Oh honey," Mrs. Zhang laughed, "Joanne at the coffee shop saw your van still parked outside this morning and mentioned it when I stopped by for my usual. Nothing stays secret in this town for more than about six hours."

"I can see that. What time do you usually get your first customers?" Janelle asked.

"Ten AM officially, but word has gotten around about today. I expect people will start showing up earlier." As if summoned by his words, they could see Jerome approaching through the front windows, practically bouncing with excitement.

"There's customer number one," Mrs. Zhang observed with amusement.

Jerome burst through the front door the moment Demetrius unlocked it, his eyes immediately going to the new displays. "Mr. D! Is this it? Is this the Black Heroes collection?"

"This is it," Demetrius confirmed, and Janelle raised her camera to capture Jerome's reaction.

"Oh wow." Jerome moved from display to display, his face lighting up with each new discovery. "Look at this one! She's a scientist and a superhero? And this guy—he looks like my cousin Marcus, but he's got powers!"

"Take your time," Demetrius said, echoing the phrase

Janelle had heard him use with young customers before. "First read is for joy."

More community members began arriving—Tia with Nevaeh, several teenagers from the group she'd seen the day before, elderly residents who seemed as curious about the comics as the children. Janelle filmed it all, capturing the genuine wonder and excitement as people discovered heroes who looked like them engaged in stories of constructive power.

"Ms. Brooks!" Tia appeared at her elbow, clutching a comic about a young girl who could communicate with animals and used her ability to solve environmental problems in her neighborhood. "This is just like my stories! She talks to animals like I talk to plants!"

"It is like your stories," Janelle agreed, crouching down to Tia's level. "What do you think about seeing someone else write the kind of hero you've been imagining?"

"It makes me feel like my ideas are good," Tia said seriously. "Like maybe other people would want to read about girls like me who have powers and use them to help."

The simple honesty of the statement made Janelle's throat tight. This was exactly what Harold had envisioned when he spent thirty years preserving these stories—children understanding that their capacity for heroism was valid and valuable.

As the morning progressed, the store filled with community members exploring Harold's collection. Janelle documented conversations between parents and children about the different kinds of heroism represented in the comics, elderly residents sharing memories of the few Black characters they'd encountered in their youth, teenagers analyzing the artistic styles and storytelling approaches.

"This is incredible," she murmured to Demetrius during a brief lull. "I've never seen a community respond to cultural materials with this level of engagement."

"That's because they're finally seeing themselves reflected in narratives of possibility instead of just survival," he replied. "Harold understood something that most of the entertainment industry still doesn't get—representation isn't just about demographics. It's about imagination. When kids can imagine themselves as heroes, they start acting heroically."

Janelle raised her camera again, filming as Jerome showed a younger boy a comic about a teenage hero who used his mathematical abilities to solve community problems. The older boy was explaining the character's problem-solving process with the enthusiasm of someone who'd found a new role model.

"That's going to be a powerful scene for the documentary," she said.

"Jerome's always been good with the younger kids. Seeing him inspired by these stories and then sharing that inspiration—it's exactly what Harold hoped would happen."

As Janelle watched Jerome mentor the younger boy, watched Tia excitedly show her discoveries to Nevaeh, watched elderly community members engage with stories that validated lifelong hopes for representation, she realized her documentary was capturing something unprecedented. This wasn't just community response to new cultural resources. This was collective transformation in real time.

And at the center of it all was Demetrius, moving through his store with quiet pride, answering questions, making connections, ensuring that Harold's thirty years of preservation work continued to fulfill its purpose of showing people what was possible when power was used constructively.

Harold's vision was alive in this room—not preserved in storage containers, but breathing, growing, inspiring the very people he'd hoped would find these stories. Janelle adjusted her camera settings and kept filming, knowing she was documenting the moment when three hundred comics stopped being a collection and became a catalyst.

CHAPTER FOURTEEN

Three days after Harold's collection arrived in Sweetgum Meadows, Demetrius found himself staying late at the store, not because he had to, but because he didn't want to leave. The past seventy-two hours had been unlike anything in his fifteen years of running Nerd Central. The store had become a gathering place in ways he'd never anticipated, with community members returning multiple times to explore different sections of the collection, to discuss the comics with friends, to share discoveries with their families.

Tonight, the store was officially closed, but Janelle was still there, reviewing footage on her laptop while sitting in the reading corner. The warm light from the desk lamp cast a golden glow over her face as she worked, occasionally pausing to make notes or adjust something on her screen. She'd been documenting the community's response with the dedication of someone who understood that she was witnessing something historically significant.

"Find anything interesting?" he asked, settling into the chair across from her with a cup of coffee.

"Everything is interesting," she said without looking up from her screen. "I've got footage of Jerome explaining *Community Heroes* to three different younger kids, each time adding new details about why the characters' problem-solving methods matter. Mrs. Washington spent an hour yesterday reading *Neighborhood Gardens* and telling anyone who'd listen about how it reminded her of her great-grand-mother's stories about community cooperation during Reconstruction."

"Mrs. Washington was here for an hour?" Demetrius hadn't noticed her staying that long, but then again, he'd been busy helping other customers navigate the collection.

"She and Mrs. Zhang got into this amazing conversation about how the comics show the same values they grew up with, just in superhero form." Janelle finally looked up from her laptop, and he caught something in her expression that looked like wonder. "They started planning a book club discussion group specifically for Harold's collection. They want to invite community members to read the comics together and talk about what they mean."

The idea made something warm spread through Demetrius's chest. This was exactly what Harold had hoped for when he'd entrusted them with his life's work—not just individual readers discovering heroes who looked like them, but community conversations about representation, hero-ism, and possibility.

"That's incredible," he said. "Did they ask you to docu-ment the discussion group?"

"They did, but they also asked if I wanted to participate

instead of just film." Janelle closed her laptop and leaned back in her chair. "I told them I'd think about it."

"What's to think about?"

"Whether I'm ready to stop being the person with the camera and start being just... a person who happens to live here."

The vulnerability in her admission made him set down his coffee cup and look at her more carefully. "Is that what you want? To just be a person who lives here?"

"I don't know," she said honestly. "For five years, I've been the documentary filmmaker who shows up, captures authentic community stories, and then leaves before anyone expects too much. It's been safe, but it's also been lonely."

"And now?"

"Now I'm living above a comic book store in a town where everyone knows where I had breakfast this morning, participating in conversations about superhero philosophy, and helping a dying man's vision come to life." She smiled, but he could see uncertainty in her eyes. "It's terrifying."

"What's terrifying about it?"

"The possibility that I might actually belong somewhere. That I might want to stay, not because I'm documenting something, but because this is where I want to build a life."

The conversation had shifted into territory that made Demetrius's chest tighten with recognition. He understood exactly what she meant—the fear that came with wanting something you'd never allowed yourself to imagine having.

"Would that be so bad?" he asked quietly.

"It would if I mess it up. If I turn out to be one of those people who's better at observing community than actually being part of it."

"You're already part of it," he said simply. "Mrs. Washington and Mrs. Zhang don't invite people to join book clubs unless they consider them community members. Jerome asks you technical questions about camera work because he thinks of you as someone who belongs here. Tia shows you her stories because she trusts you with her creativity."

"And what do you think?"

The direct question caught him off guard, and he realized that his answer mattered more than either of them had acknowledged. "I think you ended up here for a reason. Harold's collection didn't bring you to Sweetgum Meadows, but it gave you a reason to stay long enough to experience what it feels like when you stop running and let people know who you are."

Janelle was quiet for a long moment, and he could see her processing his words. When she finally spoke, her voice was softer than usual.

"Can I tell you something?"

"Of course."

"Yesterday, when I was filming Jerome and that younger boy discussing the empathy-based hero comic, I realized I wasn't just documenting their conversation—I was learning from it. Jerome was explaining how the character's ability to understand other people's emotions helped him solve conflicts without violence, and I found myself thinking about my own patterns of emotional avoidance."

"What do you mean?"

"I mean that I've spent years documenting authentic human connections while carefully avoiding forming them myself. I tell other people's stories about belonging while convincing myself that I'm too damaged by foster care to actually experience belonging."

The honesty in her admission made something shift in his chest. "And what did Jerome's explanation teach you?"

"That maybe understanding is the first step toward connection. That maybe I've been so focused on protecting myself from disappointment that I've missed opportunities for genuine relationship."

They sat in comfortable silence for a moment, the weight of the conversation settling between them. Through the store's front windows, Demetrius could see Main Street settling into its evening quiet, porch lights beginning to flicker on as Sweetgum Meadows prepared for another peaceful night.

Protecting herself from disappointment. Missing opportunities for genuine relationship. The words resonated uncomfortably because he recognized the pattern—he'd been doing the same thing for eight years, ever since Denise had left. Just with different justifications. Janelle's courage in naming her own emotional patterns made him realize that maybe it was time to be equally honest.

"Can I tell you something?" he said eventually.

"Of course."

"When I offered you the apartment, I told myself it was practical—you needed housing, I had empty space, it made sense for you to be close to the collection." He paused, choosing his words carefully. "But the truth is, I offered it because the thought of you sleeping in your van while doing this important work bothered me more than it should have if we were just professional partners."

"What are you saying?"

"I'm saying that somewhere between Memphis and here, between Harold's test and watching you document the community's response to his collection, this stopped being just a professional partnership for me."

The admission hung in the air between them, and Demetrius felt the familiar urge to retreat, to qualify the statement or make it less vulnerable. But looking at Janelle sitting in the reading corner of his store, surrounded by Harold's carefully preserved stories of constructive heroism, he realized that maybe it was time to stop protecting himself from the possibility of disappointment and start risking the possibility of connection.

"I care about you," he said simply. "Not just as a partner in preserving Harold's legacy, but as someone who's become important to me in ways I didn't expect."

Janelle's eyes were bright with something that might have been tears, but her voice was steady when she spoke. "I care about you too. More than I planned to, more than feels safe."

"So what do we do with that?"

"I don't know," she admitted. "I've never been good at staying in one place long enough to find out what 'more than caring' might look like."

"Maybe we figure it out together," Demetrius suggested. "One day at a time, like everything else that matters."

The sound of rain beginning to patter against the store's windows filled the silence that followed their admissions.

"The book club meeting is next Wednesday evening," Janelle said eventually. "Mrs. Washington wants to start with the community-building themed comics."

"Are you going to participate or document?"

"Both, maybe. I could set up a camera to capture the general discussion, but also be part of the conversation."

"That sounds like a good compromise."

"It sounds like the first step toward figuring out what I

want my life to look like when I'm not running from place to place."

Demetrius nodded, understanding exactly what she meant. They were both standing at the edge of something unfamiliar—the possibility of letting someone else matter enough to change their carefully constructed lives.

"One day at a time?" he suggested.

"One day at a time," she agreed, and for the first time since he'd met her, her smile carried no reservation at all.

Outside, the rain continued to fall over Sweetgum Meadows. Inside Nerd Central, surrounded by Harold's collection, Demetrius sat quietly with the knowledge that whatever this was between them, it had stopped being just about the comics a long time ago.

CHAPTER FIFTEEN

The phone call came at 6:15 PM, just as Janelle was setting up her camera equipment for the evening's Harold's Heroes Book Club meeting. She almost didn't answer the Memphis number, assuming it was a wrong number or telemarketer.

"Janelle Brooks."

"Ms. Brooks, this is Lena Price. Harold's neighbor." The woman's voice was thick with tears. "I wanted you to know... Harold passed away yesterday morning. Peacefully, in his sleep."

The camera tripod slipped from Janelle's suddenly nerveless fingers, clattering against the diner's floor. "What?"

"He'd been talking about you and Mr. Lakeson all week, so proud that his collection had found the right home. He asked me to call you when... when the time came. Said you'd want to know."

Demetrius looked up from where he was arranging chairs around the discussion table. "Janelle? What's wrong?"

She couldn't speak. The weight of Harold's death hit her

like a physical blow—this man who had trusted them with thirty years of his life's work, who had tested them not with questions about market value or comic book knowledge, but with questions about understanding and hope and the power of constructive heroism.

"Ms. Brooks?" Lena's voice came through the phone, concerned.

"I'm here," Janelle managed. "When is the service?"

"Saturday morning at ten. But Harold was very specific—he didn't want people mourning him. He wanted his collection celebrated. He said the real memorial would be watching young people discover heroes who looked like them."

After Lena hung up, Janelle stood frozen in the middle of Rochelle's Diner, holding her phone and trying to process the reality that Harold Murphy—the man who had made all of this possible—was gone.

"Janelle." Demetrius's voice was gentle, and suddenly he was beside her, his hand on her shoulder. "What happened?"

"Harold died yesterday." The words came out flat, emotionless. "Peacefully, in his sleep."

She watched Demetrius absorb the news, saw the same grief she was feeling reflected in his expression. Harold had been a stranger to them two weeks ago, but in that apartment bedroom in Memphis, he'd become the keeper of a vision they now shared responsibility for preserving.

"The book club," she said suddenly, looking around the diner where community members were beginning to arrive. "We can't... I can't..."

"Yes, we can," Demetrius said firmly. "Harold would want people engaging with his stories, especially tonight."

Mrs. Washington and Mrs. Zhang entered together, immediately noticing the tension in the room.

"What's wrong, dear?" Mrs. Washington asked, approaching them with concern.

"Harold Murphy, the man who collected these comics, passed away yesterday," Demetrius explained quietly.

The news rippled through the gathering community members. Jerome's excitement faded into something more solemn. Even Tia seemed to understand that someone important was gone.

"Then tonight is a memorial," Mrs. Zhang said. "A celebration of what he preserved."

"Before we begin," Mrs. Washington said, "let's take a moment to acknowledge Harold Murphy, who trusted our community with his life's work."

The silence that followed was profound. Janelle found herself thinking about the dying man who had spent thirty years hunting down stories that showed Black characters as builders and healers rather than just survivors.

"Harold would want us to discuss the stories tonight," Demetrius said eventually.

The discussion was different from their previous meetings—more thoughtful, more reverent. Community members shared not just their thoughts about the comics, but their gratitude.

"This comic about the teacher," Jerome said, holding up *Classroom Champions*, "it made me want to help other kids the way Mr. D helps us here in the store."

"I've been writing more stories since reading these," Tia added quietly. "About girls who use their powers to help their neighborhoods."

As the evening progressed, Janelle found herself filming

the way grief and gratitude could coexist in the same space. Harold's death had deepened the community's understanding of what his collection represented.

After everyone had gone home, after the equipment was packed away and the diner had returned to quiet, Janelle and Demetrius walked slowly back toward Main Street.

"I can't believe he's gone," she said finally. "Two weeks ago, I didn't even know he existed. Now it feels like I've lost someone important."

"You did lose someone important," Demetrius said quietly. "We both did. Harold wasn't just the collector—he was the keeper of a vision. And now we're responsible for that vision."

They stopped walking, standing under one of the old streetlights that cast gentle pools of light along Sweetgum Meadows' quiet streets.

"I don't know if I'm strong enough for that responsibility," Janelle admitted. "What if I can't do justice to his story in my documentary?"

"Look at what's happened in our community because you helped bring his collection here," Demetrius said, turning to face her. "Look at the discussions, the connections, the way people are thinking about heroism differently. Harold chose well when he trusted us."

The conviction in his voice broke something open in Janelle's chest. The grief she'd been holding back since Lena's phone call, the overwhelming responsibility, the fear that she would somehow fail—all of it came rushing to the surface.

She started crying, deep sobs that seemed to come from some place she'd kept locked away for years.

Without hesitation, Demetrius stepped forward and

wrapped his arms around her, pulling her against his chest while she grieved.

"It's okay," he murmured against her hair. "It's okay to be scared."

She clung to him, breathing in the familiar scent of his cologne mixed with coffee. For the first time since foster care, she let someone hold her while she fell apart.

"I don't want to leave," she whispered against his shirt. "I don't want to finish the documentary and drive away from here. But I don't know how to stay."

"What do you mean?"

"I mean I've never belonged anywhere long enough to build a life. I don't know how to be the person who stays."

Demetrius was quiet for a long moment, his arms tightening around her. When he finally spoke, his voice was rough with emotion.

"Then maybe we figure it out together," he said quietly. "I've been protecting myself from caring too much about anyone for eight years. Maybe it's time to stop being so careful."

She pulled back enough to look at his face, seeing vulnerability there that matched her own. "What are you saying?"

"I'm saying that I care about you more than I planned to. More than feels safe." He cupped her face gently, his thumb brushing away her tears. "I'm saying that the thought of you leaving, of finishing your documentary and driving away from here... it makes me realize I don't want to go back to the way things were before you came."

The admission hung between them, raw and honest. Janelle felt her heart skip, felt something that might have been hope mixing with the grief and fear.

"I don't want to leave either," she whispered. "I don't want to go back to documenting other people's lives while avoiding building my own. But I'm scared of wanting something this much."

"So am I," Demetrius said softly. "But maybe being scared together is better than being safe alone."

For a moment they just looked at each other, the space between them charged with possibility and grief and something neither of them had been brave enough to name until now. Then Demetrius leaned down, slowly, giving her time to pull away if she wanted to.

She didn't want to.

When his lips touched hers, soft and questioning, Janelle felt something fundamental shift in her chest. This wasn't the desperate kiss of people seeking distraction from pain—it was gentle, reverent, full of the careful tenderness of two people who had been protecting their hearts and were finally ready to risk them.

She responded without thinking, her hands sliding up to rest against his chest, feeling his heartbeat strong and steady beneath her palms. The kiss deepened naturally, sweetly, and she could taste the lingering coffee on his lips mixed with something that was uniquely him. His hands remained on her face, thumbs tracing gentle circles on her cheekbones, as if he was memorizing the moment.

When they finally broke apart, it was gradual, reluctant. They stayed close, foreheads nearly touching, sharing the same breath in the quiet space under the streetlight. Janelle could feel her own pulse racing, could see the same wonder in his eyes that she felt blooming in her chest.

"That was..." she started, then realized she didn't have words for what it was.

"Worth waiting for," Demetrius finished quietly, his voice rough with emotion.

They walked slowly toward her apartment above the store, not quite holding hands but close enough that their shoulders brushed with each step. The silence felt full of possibility rather than empty.

At her door, they paused. Both aware that this was a moment that would define what came next.

"I should let you get some rest," Demetrius said, though he made no move to leave. "Today has been..."

"Life-changing," she finished.

He reached out and touched her hand gently. "Are you okay? With everything that happened tonight?"

The question encompassed Harold's death, their conversation, the kiss—all wrapped up in his concern for her wellbeing.

"I'm sad about Harold," she said honestly. "But with everything else... I'm more okay than I've been in a very long time."

"Good," he said simply. "Sleep well, Janelle."

She watched him walk down the stairs and disappear around the corner, then let herself into the apartment. As she prepared for bed, Janelle found herself thinking about tomorrow—the community would continue engaging with Harold's stories, and she would be there to document it all. Not as an outsider, but as someone who belonged.

The kiss had changed something fundamental between her and Demetrius. It was about choosing to be vulnerable, choosing to build rather than protect, choosing to stay instead of run.

For the first time in her adult life, Janelle fell asleep not planning her next move, but looking forward to tomorrow in the place where she belonged.

CHAPTER SIXTEEN

Demetrius woke the next morning with the strange disorientation that came from having his world fundamentally altered in the space of a single evening. Harold was gone. He'd kissed Janelle under a streetlight. She'd said she didn't want to leave. The memory of her response to his kiss, the way she'd melted against him with a soft sigh that suggested she'd been waiting for that moment as much as he had—it all felt simultaneously surreal and like the most natural thing that had ever happened.

He arrived at the store earlier than usual, needing the familiar routine of opening up, checking inventory, organizing displays. But even the mundane tasks felt different now. The apartment above his head wasn't just storage space —it was where Janelle was sleeping, probably still in the soft pajamas he'd glimpsed when she answered her door. The reading corner where she often sat reviewing footage carried the faint scent of her shampoo. Everything felt charged with new meaning.

At eight-thirty, he heard movement upstairs—the soft

pad of feet across the floor, water running in the kitchen. The sounds of her morning routine made something warm settle in his chest, a domestic intimacy he hadn't experienced in years.

When she appeared at the connecting door twenty minutes later, carrying two cups of coffee and wearing jeans and a sweater that made her look soft and approachable, he felt his pulse quicken in a way that had nothing to do with caffeine deprivation.

"Good morning," she said, and there was a slight shyness in her voice that hadn't been there before last night.

"Morning." He accepted the coffee gratefully, hyper-aware when their fingers brushed. "How did you sleep?"

"Better than I expected, considering everything." She settled into the reading corner chair, tucking one leg beneath her. "I kept thinking about Harold, but also about... everything else."

The "everything else" hung between them, encompassing the kiss, their admissions, the shift from careful friendship to something that felt both fragile and inevitable.

"Any regrets?" he asked, then immediately wished he hadn't. It was too direct, too vulnerable, too much like asking for reassurance he had no right to demand.

But Janelle smiled, the first genuinely relaxed expression he'd seen from her since Lena's phone call. "About Harold dying, yes. About last night between us? Not one."

The relief that flooded through him was disproportionate to the simple words, but he realized he'd been holding his breath since he'd left her at her door, wondering if the morning light would bring second thoughts or professional distance.

"I should probably call Lena today," Janelle continued.

"Find out more details about Harold's service, see if there's anything we can do to honor his wishes about celebrating the collection instead of mourning him."

"We could organize something here," Demetrius suggested. "A community reading, maybe. People sharing their favorite Harold comics and what they meant to them."

"That's perfect. He wanted his real memorial to be watching young people discover heroes who looked like them. We could document the community's response to his collection as a living tribute."

The way she said "we" made something settle more deeply in his chest. They were planning together, thinking beyond the immediate grief and attraction to what they could build as partners in preserving Harold's legacy.

The bell above the door chimed, and Jerome entered with his usual morning energy, though there was something subdued about his expression.

"Mr. D," he said, approaching the counter. "I've been thinking about the memorial service we talked about last night. I have some ideas."

"That's great, Jerome. What were you thinking?"

Jerome considered his words carefully. "I think he'd want us to talk about the stories he saved. Like, maybe people could read their favorite parts out loud? And kids could share drawings they made based on the characters?"

"Those are wonderful ideas," Janelle said, pulling out her notebook. "Would you be willing to help organize something like that?"

"Really? You'd want me to help plan it?"

"Jerome, you understand these comics as well as anyone," Demetrius said. "Harold would have loved having young people take the lead in celebrating his work."

As Jerome left to spread the word among his friends, Demetrius found himself watching Janelle organize notes about the memorial service. There was something different about the way she moved through the space now—less like a visitor documenting an interesting community and more like someone making plans for her own life.

"Can I ask you something?" he said during a quiet moment between customers.

"Of course."

"Last night you said you didn't know how to be the person who stays. But you've been part of this community for weeks now. Everyone already thinks of you as belonging here."

Janelle was quiet for a moment, twisting a strand of hair around her finger. "There's a difference between being welcomed somewhere and believing you have the right to stay permanently. I've been good at being a grateful guest, but I've never had to figure out how to be a neighbor, a partner, a... whatever this is we're becoming."

"What do you think we're becoming?"

"I don't know exactly. But I know it feels important in a way that scares me." She looked at him directly. "I've spent my whole adult life being able to leave whenever things got complicated. Now I'm in a situation where I don't want to leave, but I also don't know how to stay without messing it up."

The honesty in her admission made him want to close the distance between them, to reassure her with touch and proximity. But they were in the store, and the morning customers were beginning to trickle in, and he sensed that pushing too hard too fast would send her back into the protective shell she'd been learning to shed.

"Maybe messing up is part of it," he said instead. "Part of building something real instead of something perfect."

"Is that what we're doing? Building something real?"

"I'd like to be."

The simple admission hung between them as Mrs. Zhang entered the store, carrying what looked like a casserole dish covered with aluminum foil.

"I brought lunch," she announced, setting the dish on the counter. "Figured you both might be too distracted to eat properly after yesterday's news."

"Mrs. Zhang, you didn't have to—" Demetrius began.

"Of course I did. Harold Murphy trusted you with thirty years of his life's work. The least I can do is make sure you're fed while you figure out how to honor that trust." She turned to Janelle with a knowing smile. "Besides, you look like you could use some of my grandmother's comfort food recipe."

As Mrs. Zhang bustled around the store, checking on the Harold collection displays and chatting with browsing customers, Demetrius caught Janelle watching the older woman with something that looked like wonder.

"She takes care of everyone," Janelle observed quietly.

"That's what community looks like," Demetrius said. "People taking care of each other not because they have to, but because that's how you build something that lasts."

"And you think I could learn to be part of that?"

"I think you already are part of it. Mrs. Zhang doesn't bring casseroles to visitors. She brings them to people she's decided belong to this place."

The afternoon brought a steady stream of community members wanting to talk about Harold, to share their thoughts about the memorial service, to browse the collection with new reverence knowing its creator was gone. Demetrius found himself watching Janelle navigate these conversations—no longer the documentarian capturing authentic community responses, but a community member herself, someone people came to for comfort and planning and shared grief.

Around three o'clock, Tia appeared with Nevaeh, clutching a folded piece of paper.

"Ms. Brooks," Tia said shyly, "I wrote something about Mr. Murphy. For the memorial service, if you want to use it."

"I'd love to hear it," Janelle said, crouching down to Tia's level.

Tia unfolded the paper and began reading in her clear, serious voice: "Mr. Murphy saved stories about heroes who look like me. He didn't know me, but he made sure I could find stories about girls who have powers and use them to help their neighborhoods. Now when I write my own stories, I remember that Mr. Murphy believed girls like me could be heroes too."

The simple tribute made Demetrius's throat tight. This was exactly what Harold had hoped for—young people understanding that they were part of a tradition of heroic representation, that their stories mattered, that their capacity for constructive power deserved to be celebrated.

"That's beautiful, Tia," Janelle said, her voice catching slightly. "Harold would have been so proud to hear that."

As the afternoon wore on, plans for Harold's memorial began to take shape. Jerome was organizing readings by young people. Mrs. Washington and Mrs. Zhang were coordinating food. Several teenagers were working on art projects inspired by their favorite Harold comics. The whole community was coming together to celebrate the man who had preserved stories of constructive heroism.

"This is what he wanted," Janelle said as they watched the planning unfold. "Not people mourning him, but people celebrating what he made possible."

"And you're documenting all of it."

"I'm participating in all of it," she corrected. "The documenting is secondary now."

The distinction felt significant. When Harold had first entrusted them with his collection, Janelle had been a documentary filmmaker helping to bring his vision to the community. Now she was a community member who happened to have documentary skills that could serve the collective effort to honor Harold's legacy.

As closing time approached and the last customers left the store, Demetrius found himself reluctant to end the day. Not because of the memorial planning or the community response, but because it meant saying goodnight to Janelle, returning to the careful distance that seemed impossible to maintain after last night.

"Would you like to have dinner?" he asked as she packed up her camera equipment. "Nothing fancy. Mrs. Zhang left enough food for an army."

"I'd like that," she said, and the simple acceptance felt like another small step toward whatever they were building together.

They ate in the store's reading corner, sharing Mrs. Zhang's casserole and talking about Harold, about the memorial plans, about the way grief and hope could coexist in the same space. The conversation felt different from their previous interactions—more intimate, more personal, as if last night's kiss had given them permission to stop being quite so careful with each other.

"Can I tell you something?" Janelle said as they finished eating.

"Always."

"I called my documentary editor this morning. Told her I was expanding the project, that it was becoming something bigger than I'd originally planned."

"What did she say?"

"She wanted to know if I was staying in Sweetgum Meadows permanently or just extending the project timeline." Janelle was quiet for a moment. "I told her I was still figuring that out."

"And what's helping you figure it out?"

"This," she said, gesturing around the store, toward the displays of Harold's collection, toward the evidence of community engagement that surrounded them. "Today, watching people plan Harold's memorial, being part of it instead of just documenting it—it felt like home in a way I've never experienced."

"But you're still scared."

"Terrified. What if I'm not as good at belonging as I am at observing? What if I disappoint people who've been kind enough to welcome me?"

Demetrius reached across the small space between their chairs and took her hand, feeling the slight tremor in her fingers that suggested her calm exterior was covering much deeper anxiety.

"What if you're exactly what this community needs? What if Harold's collection brought you here not just to document the story, but to become part of it?"

"And what about us?" she asked quietly. "What if I stay and we try this and it doesn't work? What if caring about each other isn't enough to build something lasting?"

"Then we'll figure it out as we go," he said simply. "Like everything else that matters."

When she smiled at that, he felt something settle more permanently in his chest. They were taking it one day at a time, one honest conversation at a time, one small risk at a time. It wasn't the dramatic romance of movies or novels, but it was real, and it was theirs.

Harold's collection had brought them together, but what they were building now was about more than preserving stories of constructive heroism. It was about choosing to be constructive heroes themselves—people who used their abilities to build communities, to support each other, to create something meaningful that could last.

As they cleaned up from dinner and prepared to say goodnight, Demetrius found himself looking forward to tomorrow not just because of the memorial planning, but because it would be another day of figuring out how to belong to each other and to this place they were both learning to call home.

CHAPTER SEVENTEEN

The memorial service for Harold took place on Saturday afternoon in the town square, with the gazebo decorated in comic book pages blown up and mounted on poster boards—panels showing heroes healing, building, teaching, and bringing communities together. The weather cooperated with clear skies and gentle warmth, as if even nature wanted to honor Harold's wish for celebration rather than mourning.

Janelle moved through the crowd with her camera, but for the first time since arriving in Sweetgum Meadows, she found herself setting it down frequently to actually participate in conversations rather than just document them. She hugged Mrs. Washington when the elderly woman teared up during Jerome's reading. She helped Tia adjust the microphone when the little girl shared her tribute. She laughed with genuine delight when several teenagers performed dramatic readings of fight scenes where heroes resolved conflicts through communication rather than violence.

"This is beautiful," Demetrius said, appearing beside

her as the formal program concluded and people began mingling around the food tables. "Harold would have loved seeing his collection bring people together like this."

"Look at Jerome," Janelle said, nodding toward where the teenager was showing a group of younger kids how to draw some of the characters from Harold's comics. "He's become such a leader."

"You helped with that. Asking him to help plan the memorial, treating his ideas as valuable—that gave him confidence to step up."

The compliment made her chest warm, but it was the way Demetrius was looking at her that made her pulse quicken. There was something different in his expression today, an intensity that suggested their careful friendship had shifted into territory that felt both thrilling and slightly dangerous.

"Ms. Brooks?" Tia tugged at her sleeve, breaking the moment. "Uncle Sean wants to know if you're going to film the dance tonight."

"What dance?"

"Didn't anyone tell you?" Demetrius's voice carried amusement. "Sweetgum Meadows has a tradition. After community events, we clear the center of the square and Sean provides music from his dance studio sound system. Everyone dances until the fireflies come out."

The image of couples swaying under the town square's string lights while fireflies blinked in the gathering dusk made something flutter in Janelle's stomach. "That sounds lovely."

"You should dance with Mr. D," Tia announced with the confidence of a nine-year-old who hadn't learned that some observations were better kept to oneself. "You like each other. I can tell."

Heat rose in Janelle's face, but before she could figure out how to respond to Tia's matchmaking, Nevaeh appeared and gently guided her niece toward the dessert table.

"Sorry about that," she called back with a grin. "Tia's been watching too many romantic comedies with her grandmother."

When they were alone again, Demetrius moved closer, close enough that she could smell his cologne and feel the warmth radiating from his skin. "For what it's worth, she's not wrong about the liking each other part."

The directness of the comment, delivered in his low voice while they stood in the middle of a community celebration, made her breath catch. This was different from their careful conversations over the past few days. This felt like flirtation, like a man who had decided to stop being quite so cautious about expressing his interest.

"Demetrius..."

"Dance with me tonight?" he asked, and there was something in his voice that suggested he was asking for more than just a dance.

"I'm not very good at it."

"Neither am I. We can figure it out together."

The words echoed their conversation from the night Harold died, when he'd suggested they figure out their relationship together instead of protecting themselves separately. But this time, the context was lighter, more playful, charged with the kind of anticipation that made her aware of every place their bodies might touch during a slow dance.

"Okay," she said, and his smile in response made her feel slightly dizzy.

The rest of the afternoon passed in a blur of conversations with community members, documentation of the memorial's impact, and an undercurrent of awareness that kept drawing her attention back to Demetrius. She found herself noticing the way he moved through the crowd, the careful attention he paid to elderly residents who wanted to share memories, the patience he showed with children who pestered him with questions about comic book characters.

By the time evening approached and Sean began setting up his sound system, Janelle's nerves were humming with anticipation. She'd changed into a sundress—one of the few non-professional pieces of clothing she'd packed—and let her hair down from its usual ponytail. Looking at herself in the bathroom mirror, she realized she looked like someone preparing for a date, not someone documenting community traditions.

The thought should have been alarming. Instead, it felt like another small step toward becoming the person who stayed instead of the person who observed and left.

The dancing began as the sun set, with older couples taking the floor first, moving to music that ranged from classic soul to contemporary R & B. Mrs. Washington and Mr. Peterson, who apparently had been dance partners for decades, demonstrated moves that had the younger crowd cheering and applauding.

Janelle stood at the edge of the impromptu dance floor, camera in hand but forgotten as she watched couples of all ages move together under the string lights Sean had arranged around the gazebo. The whole scene felt like something out of a movie—magical and slightly surreal.

"Still planning to document instead of participate?"

Demetrius's voice was warm with amusement as he appeared beside her.

"I was just..."

"Overthinking it?"

She looked at him and felt her resolve crumble. He'd changed clothes too, trading his usual button-down shirt for something softer, more casual. His sleeves were rolled up, revealing strong forearms, and there was something different about his whole posture—more relaxed, more confident, like a man who had decided to take some risks.

"Maybe a little."

"Come on," he said, extending his hand. "One dance. If you hate it, I promise to let you go back to hiding behind your camera."

She set the camera on a nearby table and took his hand, letting him lead her onto the makeshift dance floor. The song playing was slow, something soulful and romantic that seemed designed to encourage close dancing.

When Demetrius pulled her against him, one hand settling at her waist and the other holding hers, Janelle felt a shock of awareness travel through her entire body. This was different from their brief kisses under the streetlight. This was sustained physical contact, intimate and deliberate.

"How am I doing so far?" she asked, trying to cover her nervousness with humor.

"Perfect," he said, his voice rougher than usual. "Just follow my lead."

But following his lead meant moving closer, meant feeling the solid warmth of his chest against hers, meant being surrounded by his scent and the gentle pressure of his hand at the small of her back. When he spun her gently and pulled her back against him, she laughed despite her nervousness, and felt some of the tension leave her shoulders.

"You're a better dancer than you claimed," she said, tilting her head back to look at him.

"You're a better partner than you feared," he replied, and there was something in his eyes that made her breath catch.

The song shifted to something even slower, and without discussion, they moved closer together. Janelle let her free hand rest on his shoulder, felt the muscle there shift as he adjusted his hold on her. They were barely dancing now, more like swaying together, lost in their own private world despite being surrounded by other couples.

"Janelle," he said quietly, and when she looked up at him, she saw her own desire reflected in his expression.

"Yeah?"

"I'm falling in love with you."

The words hit her like a physical shock, not because they were unwelcome, but because they named something she'd been feeling but hadn't been brave enough to acknowledge. The careful boundaries they'd been maintaining, the gradual building of trust and attraction, the way he'd become the first person she'd ever wanted to stay for—all of it crystallized into something that felt both inevitable and miraculous.

"I'm falling in love with you too," she whispered, and saw something like relief and joy transform his features.

He stopped moving entirely then, cupping her face in both hands while other couples continued dancing around them. "Can I kiss you?"

"Please."

When his lips met hers this time, it wasn't gentle or questioning like their first kiss had been. This was heat and certainty and months of careful attraction finally given permission to burn freely. She melted against him, her hands fisting in his shirt, and heard him make a low sound of approval that sent fire shooting through her veins.

When they finally broke apart, both breathing hard, Janelle realized they'd drawn some amused attention from nearby dancers.

"Maybe we should..."

"Continue this somewhere more private?" he finished, his voice rough with want.

"Your place or mine?" she asked, then flushed at her own boldness.

His smile was pure masculine satisfaction. "Yours is closer."

The walk back to her apartment above the store felt both endless and too short. They didn't speak, but his hand in hers felt like a promise, and the tension building between them made the air feel electric with possibility.

At her door, they paused, both aware that crossing this threshold would change everything between them.

"Are you sure?" Demetrius asked, ever careful of her feelings even in the midst of obvious desire.

"I've never been more sure of anything," she said honestly.

When she unlocked the door and led him inside, Janelle felt a certainty settle over her that she'd never experienced before. This wasn't just about physical attraction or the romance of dancing under the stars. This was about choosing to be vulnerable with someone who had proven himself worthy of that trust, about building something real with a man who understood both her fears and her dreams.

The apartment felt different with him in it—smaller, more intimate. Moonlight streamed through the windows, casting everything in soft silver light that made the moment feel dreamlike.

Demetrius turned to face her, his hands coming up to frame her face with a gentleness that made her heart race. "Are you sure about this?"

Instead of answering with words, she rose on her toes and kissed him, pouring all her certainty and want into the connection between them. He responded immediately, his arms coming around her, pulling her closer until there was no space left between them.

When they broke apart, both breathing hard, his forehead rested against hers. "Janelle..."

"I know," she whispered. "I feel it too."

He kissed her again, deeper this time, and she felt herself melting against him. His hands were warm and sure as they traced the line of her spine, and when she sighed into his mouth, she felt his response in the way his arms tightened around her.

"I've wanted this," she admitted against his lips. "Wanted you. For longer than I was brave enough to admit."

"So have I," he said, his voice rough with emotion and desire. "Every day, watching you become part of this community, part of my life..."

She took his hand and led him toward the bedroom, her heart hammering but her resolve steady. At the threshold, she turned back to him, seeing her own wonder reflected in his eyes.

"I've never felt like this before," she said softly. "Like I belong somewhere completely."

"You belong here," he said, his thumb tracing the line of her cheek. "With me. With this community. You belong, Janelle."

When he kissed her this time, it was with a reverence that made tears prick her eyes. This wasn't just passion—it was recognition, acceptance, love in its purest form.

MUCH LATER, as they lay entwined in the soft darkness, Demetrius traced lazy patterns on her bare shoulder. "No regrets?"

"None," she said, pressing a kiss to his chest where her head rested. "You?"

"Only that it took us this long to get here."

She lifted her head to look at him, seeing contentment and love in his expression. "We got here when we were ready. When we were both brave enough."

"I love you," he said simply, and the words felt like coming home.

"I love you too," she replied, and meant it with every fiber of her being.

As she drifted toward sleep in his arms, Janelle realized that Harold's collection had given them more than just stories of constructive heroism. It had given them the framework for building their own love story—one based on mutual support, shared values, and the courage to be vulnerable with someone who would cherish that vulnerability.

She was home. Finally, completely, home.

CHAPTER EIGHTEEN

Demetrius woke gradually, awareness returning in layers. First came the unfamiliar softness of Janelle's bed, then the warm weight of her curled against his side, her hair tickling his chest where her head rested. Early morning light filtered through her curtains, casting everything in golden hues that made the moment feel suspended in amber.

He'd stayed the night. And now she was sleeping peacefully in his arms, her breathing steady and calm, as if having him there was the most natural thing in the world.

The significance of it made his chest tight with emotion. For eight years, he'd convinced himself that solitude was safer than vulnerability, that serving his community was enough, that he didn't need the complications of intimate partnership. Now, holding Janelle as she slept, he wondered how he'd survived so long without this feeling of completeness.

She stirred against him, making a soft sound of contentment that went straight to his heart.

"Good morning," she murmured without opening her eyes, her hand finding his chest and resting there as if claiming him.

"Good morning, beautiful."

That made her eyes flutter open, and the smile that spread across her face was soft and slightly shy—so different from the confident documentarian he'd first met. This was Janelle without any armor, trusting and vulnerable and completely his.

"How are you feeling?" he asked, needing to know she had no regrets about crossing this line with him.

"Like I finally understand what all those love songs are about," she said, her honesty making him laugh. "And slightly nervous about facing the town later. Small communities talk, don't they?"

"They do. But not meanly. More like... invested in each other's happiness." He traced a finger along her bare shoulder, marveling at his right to touch her like this. "Mrs. Zhang will probably show up with celebratory casseroles."

"Oh God," Janelle groaned, burying her face against his neck. "How mortifying."

"Or endearing. She's been dropping not-so-subtle hints about us for weeks."

"Has she really?"

"Asked me three times if you were 'settling in well' and whether I was 'taking proper care of our guest.' Which, knowing Mrs. Zhang, was less about hospitality and more about matchmaking."

Janelle lifted her head to look at him, and he caught something shifting in her expression. "About that. About being a guest, I mean."

His chest tightened. "What about it?"

"I need to make some decisions. About my documentary timeline, about my living situation, about..." She gestured between them. "About what this means for my future."

The practical realities they'd been avoiding couldn't be pushed aside indefinitely. Janelle's project had a scope and timeline. She had a career and a life beyond Sweetgum Meadows, even if that life had been uncertain when she'd arrived. Last night had been about love and connection, but this morning required conversations about logistics and long-term planning.

"What are you thinking?" he asked carefully.

"I'm thinking I want to stay. Not just extend the documentary timeline, but actually stay. Make Sweetgum Meadows my home base, build a life here." She paused, vulnerability flickering across her features. "With you, if you want that."

Relief flooded through him so intensely it was almost overwhelming. "Of course I want that. But are you sure? Your career, your independence—"

"My career can be based anywhere I have good internet and a willingness to travel when necessary. And my independence... I'm learning that independence and interdependence aren't mutually exclusive." She traced patterns on his chest as she spoke. "I can belong somewhere without losing myself. I can build a life with someone without giving up my ambitions."

"The documentary?"

"Will be better because I stayed. Because I documented not just the initial community response to Harold's collection, but the long-term impact. Because I can show what happens when someone stops running and chooses to build something lasting."

The way she said it made him think she was talking about more than just professional choices. "And what about the practical details? Money, housing, work arrangements?"

"That's the scary part. I still don't have much money, and I'll need to find sustainable income while I work on the expanded documentary." She traced patterns on his chest as she spoke. "I can freelance, maybe teach some documentary workshops. And I'll be able to pitch this project for a much higher fee now that it's evolved into something more comprehensive. But the housing situation..."

"Move in with me," he said simply.

She lifted her head to look at him. "Demetrius, I can't ask you to—"

"You're not asking. I'm offering. I have a house with plenty of space, and I'd love nothing more than to wake up next to you every morning." His voice grew more serious. "I know it's fast, but after everything we've been through, everything we've built together... I can't imagine wanting anyone else sharing my space. My life."

"Are you sure? That's a big step."

"I'm sure. You can keep this apartment as your office space for the documentary work. You'll have room to spread out equipment, do interviews, edit footage. And my house..." He smiled. "My house has been waiting for someone to make it feel like a home instead of just a place I sleep."

When they broke apart, both breathless and laughing, Janelle settled back against his chest with a contentment he could feel in her entire body.

"There's something else," she said quietly. "About the documentary. I want to expand it beyond just Harold's collection. I want to document the whole community—the businesses, the traditions, the way people here have built something lasting and inclusive. Make Sweetgum Meadows a case study in authentic community building."

"That sounds like a multi-year project."

"It does, doesn't it?" Her voice carried satisfaction rather than concern. "Good thing I'll be living with you."

They lay together in comfortable silence for a while, processing the shift from uncertainty to commitment, from careful dating to life partnership. It felt enormous and natural at the same time, like the culmination of a story they'd been writing together without realizing it.

"I should probably head home and change clothes before the store opens," Demetrius said eventually, though he made no move to leave her arms.

"Trying to maintain some dignity after our very public display last night?" Janelle asked with amusement.

"Something like that. Though I suspect the whole town already knows exactly how we feel about each other."

"And where you spent the night," Janelle added with a laugh. "Mrs. Zhang probably saw the lights in your house stay off all night."

"Jerome will be insufferably smug about being right about us," Demetrius said. "That kid's been predicting this for weeks."

"Are you complaining?" she asked.

"Never," he said firmly, then leaned down for another kiss that made leaving even more difficult.

Eventually, practical necessity won out over romantic inclination. Demetrius extracted himself from Janelle's bed and arms, though not without significant reluctance and promises to return later with dinner and plans for the evening.

As he walked home through Sweetgum Meadows' quiet

morning streets, he found himself noticing details he'd taken for granted for fifteen years. The way morning light painted the old houses golden. The sound of church bells beginning to ring across town. The elderly couples already working in their front gardens, waving as he passed.

This was his community, his home, the place he'd chosen to build his life. And now Janelle had chosen it too. Not just as a temporary assignment or professional opportunity, but as the place where she wanted to belong permanently.

The thought made him want to run back to her apartment, to wake her with kisses and coffee and plans for their shared future. Instead, he let himself into his own house—which suddenly felt too empty, too quiet, too much like the careful solitude he'd maintained for too many years.

By the time he'd showered and changed and walked back to open Nerd Central, his mind was already racing with possibilities. Janelle's expanded documentary project would require coordination with local businesses, interviews with longtime residents, documentation of community events and traditions. She'd need local connections, introductions, logistical support.

She'd need a partner who understood the community and could help her navigate the relationships that would make her project successful. Not just a romantic partner, but a collaborator who shared her vision and could contribute to the work in meaningful ways.

As he unlocked the store and began his Sunday morning routine, Demetrius realized that Harold's collection had given them more than just the catalyst for their relationship. It had provided a model for partnership—two people with complementary skills working together to preserve and share something valuable, supporting each other's strengths while creating something neither could accomplish alone.

He was just finishing the opening checklist when Jerome arrived, as predicted, with the enthusiasm he brought to all things comic-related.

"Mr. D! Did you see Ms. Brooks this morning? I knocked on her door upstairs to ask about filming the memorial service yesterday, but she didn't answer. Her van's still here, so I know she didn't leave town."

Demetrius managed to keep his expression neutral, though Jerome's innocent question made him acutely aware of how their relationship had shifted overnight. "She might still be sleeping. Yesterday was a long day for everyone."

"True. The memorial was really beautiful. Based on everything you and Ms. Brooks told us about him, I think Harold would have loved it." Jerome paused in his inventory sorting to grin at him. "So, Mr. D, that was quite a kiss you and Ms. Brooks shared at the dance last night. Pretty much the whole town saw it."

Demetrius felt heat rise in his face but couldn't help smiling. "I guess we weren't exactly subtle."

"Not even close. But everyone's happy for you. We've all been hoping you'd finally make a move." Jerome's grin widened. "So are you going to ask her to stay? Permanently, I mean? She fits here, you know? And you seem happier when she's around."

The observation from a fifteen-year-old made Demetrius realize their connection had been obvious to the community long before they'd admitted it to themselves. "Why do you ask?"

"Because she makes you smile more. And she's not just documenting us anymore—she's part of us. Like, really part of us. And..." Jerome hesitated, then pushed forward with teenage honesty. "And I think you love her."

The simple statement, delivered without drama or embarrassment, made Demetrius's chest tighten with affection for the boy who'd become like family to him over the years.

"Yes," he said quietly. "I do love her."

"And she loves you too. Anyone can see it." Jerome grinned. "So when are you asking her to stay?"

"She's already decided to stay," Demetrius said, unable to keep the satisfaction out of his voice.

Jerome's whoop of joy could probably be heard three blocks away. "Really? She's staying for good?"

"For good."

"That's awesome! Wait until I tell everyone. Mrs. Zhang is going to be so happy she'll probably cook for the entire town." Jerome paused in his celebration. "This means you're going to be together, right? Like, officially together?"

"Officially together," Demetrius confirmed, and saying it out loud made it feel even more real.

As Jerome launched into plans for how the community should celebrate this development—suggestions that ranged from sensible (a welcome party) to ambitious (renaming a street in Janelle's honor)—Demetrius found himself thinking about the future he and Janelle would build together.

Their relationship had started with a professional partnership around Harold's collection, but it had grown into something much deeper. They shared values, complementary skills, and a vision for how communities could support individual growth while fostering collective wellbeing. They could build something together that would serve both their professional ambitions and their personal happiness.

Harold's stories of constructive heroism had brought them together, but their love story was entirely their own—full of the kind of everyday heroism that built lasting relationships and stronger communities.

As the morning progressed and regular customers began arriving, Demetrius found himself watching for Janelle's appearance, eager to see her in daylight as his partner rather than his careful friend. When she finally came downstairs around ten-thirty, carrying coffee and wearing a sundress that made her look soft and radiant, his heart did something athletic in his chest.

"Good morning," she said, and though her greeting was casual, her eyes held memories of the night before and promises for the future.

"Good morning," he replied, and knew that every morning that started this way would be a gift.

They had work to do—a documentary to complete, a community to serve, a relationship to build day by day. But for the first time in his adult life, Demetrius had the certainty that he was building something meaningful with someone who understood his dreams, in a place where they both belonged, surrounded by people who had already welcomed them home.

Three months after Harold's memorial service, Janelle woke in Demetrius's arms on a crisp September morning, sunlight streaming through the curtains of the house that had become theirs. The transition from living above the store to sharing his home had been seamless in ways that still surprised her—no awkward negotiations about space or routines, just the natural rhythm of two people who had somehow been designed to fit together.

"Morning, beautiful," Demetrius murmured against her hair, his voice still rough with sleep.

"Morning yourself." She turned in his arms, marveling as she did every day at the simple luxury of waking up next to someone who loved her completely. "Ready for the Fall Harvest Festival setup?"

"As ready as anyone can be for Mrs. Washington's organizational prowess." He pressed a kiss to her forehead. "She had me moving apple barrels until nine last night."

Janelle laughed, remembering the controlled chaos of the previous evening. The Fall Harvest Festival was Sweetgum

Meadows' biggest autumn celebration, and Mrs. Washington had appointed herself chief coordinator with the efficiency of a military general. Janelle had spent the evening documenting the setup process, watching community members transform the town square into an autumnal wonderland.

"I need to get some footage of the early morning prep before people start arriving," she said, already mentally organizing her shot list. "The way the light hits those pumpkin displays is perfect right now."

"Always working," Demetrius teased, but his tone was fond rather than critical. He understood her need to capture moments, just as she understood his dedication to serving their community.

"Speaking of work, didn't you promise Jerome you'd help set up the comic book booth?"

The Fall Harvest Festival had become an opportunity for local businesses to showcase their offerings, and Jerome had convinced Demetrius to create a display featuring Harold's collection alongside traditional autumn-themed comics. It was exactly the kind of community engagement Harold would have loved—his carefully preserved stories reaching new readers during a celebration of harvest and abundance.

An hour later, Janelle made her way down Main Street with her camera, documenting the festival's transformation of their usually quiet town. Vendors were arranging displays of local crafts and seasonal goods, while the aroma of apple cider and pumpkin spice drifted from Roasted Beans Coffee Spot's festival booth. The entire town square had been decorated with barrels of apples, stacks of hay, and garlands of autumn leaves that created a picture-perfect backdrop for the day's festivities.

"Ms. Brooks! Ms. Brooks!" Tia came running toward her,

practically vibrating with excitement. "Did you see the pumpkin display? Uncle Sean helped me pick the perfect one for carving later!"

"I can't wait to film that," Janelle said, crouching down to Tia's level. "Have you decided what design you're going to carve?"

"A girl with superpowers helping her community," Tia announced proudly. "Just like the heroes in Mr. Harold's comics."

The simple statement made Janelle's chest tighten with gratitude. Three months since Harold's death, and his influence continued to ripple through the community in ways both large and small. Tia's pumpkin design was just one example of how his vision of constructive heroism had taken root in Sweetgum Meadows.

"That sounds perfect," Janelle said. "Harold would have loved that."

As the morning progressed, Janelle found herself moving through the festival not just as a documentarian, but as a genuine participant. She helped Mrs. Zhang arrange her booth of autumn-themed baked goods, cheered for contestants in the apple pie baking contest, and laughed with genuine delight when Demetrius got roped into the hayride tour of town.

"You're not filming this," he called to her as the hay-filled wagon bounced down Main Street, his expression a mix of embarrassment and amusement.

"I'm absolutely filming this!" she called back, raising her camera with a grin.

This was what she'd learned to love about small-town life —the way everyone was expected to participate, to contribute, to be part of the fabric of community rather than just observers. For someone who had spent years documenting other people's lives while carefully maintaining her own distance, the integration had been both challenging and deeply rewarding.

Around noon, as the festival reached its peak energy, Janelle found herself at Jerome's comic book booth, filming him as he introduced younger children to Harold's collection.

"This one's about a girl who can grow anything," Jerome was explaining to a group of fascinated eight-year-olds. "She uses her powers to help her neighborhood create community gardens and solve food problems. See how she's not fighting anyone? She's building something."

"Just like our school garden project!" one of the children exclaimed.

"Exactly like that," Jerome confirmed, and Janelle could hear the pride in his voice—not just in the comic, but in making the connection between Harold's stories and real-world community action.

As she filmed, Janelle caught sight of Demetrius watching from the edge of the booth, his expression soft with something that looked like wonder. When their eyes met, he mouthed "I love you," and she felt that familiar flutter of gratitude for the life they'd built together.

"Ms. Janelle," Mrs. Washington appeared beside her with a plate of festival food. "You've been working all morning. Time to eat something and enjoy the celebration."

It was a gentle but firm instruction, the kind Mrs. Washington had been giving her for months—reminders that she was part of the community now, not just its documentarian. Janelle accepted the plate gratefully, noting how natural it felt to be taken care of by the community elders.

"How's the documentary coming along?" Mrs. Washington asked as they found a spot to sit in the shade.

"Better than I ever imagined," Janelle said honestly. "It started as a story about Harold's collection, but it's become something bigger. A story about how communities preserve not just objects, but values. How they pass on wisdom about what it means to use power constructively."

"And what about you?" Mrs. Washington's eyes twinkled with the knowing look of someone who had watched many young people find their way home. "How are you settling in?"

Janelle looked around the festival—at Jerome teaching children about heroism, at Demetrius helping elderly residents navigate the crowded booths, at Tia showing off her pumpkin selection to anyone who would listen. This was her community now, these were her people, and for the first time in her adult life, she felt completely certain about where she belonged.

"I'm not settling in anymore," she said with a smile. "I'm home."

The afternoon brought the highlight of the festival—the pumpkin carving contest. Janelle documented families working together on elaborate designs, teenagers attempting complex patterns, and elderly residents sharing techniques they'd learned decades ago. But the moment that made her heart swell was watching Tia carefully carve her superhero pumpkin, tongue poking out in concentration as she brought her vision to life.

"It's perfect," Demetrius said, appearing beside Janelle as they watched Tia add finishing touches to her creation.

"It really is." Janelle lowered her camera, content to simply experience the moment rather than capture it.

"Harold would have been so proud to see his influence spreading like this."

"He would have been proud of you too," Demetrius said quietly. "For the way you've helped his vision reach even more people."

As evening approached and the festival began to wind down, Janelle found herself reflecting on the changes in her life since arriving in Sweetgum Meadows. The scared, financially desperate woman who had driven eight hours on a stranger's phone call felt like a different person entirely. That woman had been running from disappointment and failure. This woman was building something lasting with someone who understood both her fears and her dreams.

The festival concluded with the traditional outdoor movie night, families spreading blankets in the town square while a classic film played on a large screen set up near the gazebo. Janelle and Demetrius settled on their own blanket, her head on his shoulder as they watched the movie under a canopy of stars.

"Thank you," she whispered during a quiet moment in the film.

"For what?"

"For helping me understand the difference between observing community and being part of it."

Demetrius pressed a kiss to the top of her head. "Thank you for choosing to stay long enough to learn the difference."

As the movie played and the community settled into the peaceful rhythm of evening, Janelle realized that her documentary was nearly complete. She had enough footage to tell Harold's story, to show how his collection had impacted Sweetgum Meadows, and to explore the broader themes of representation and community building that his work embodied.

But more importantly, she had found the story of her own transformation—from observer to participant, from documenter to community member, from someone who recorded other people's homes to someone who had finally found her own.

The documentary would be her gift to Harold's memory and her tribute to the community that had welcomed her. But the life she'd built here, the love she'd found with Demetrius, the sense of belonging that had grown from their shared commitment to serving something larger than themselves—that was her gift to herself.

Harold's collection had brought them together, but what they'd created was entirely their own. And tomorrow, she would begin the final phase of editing, preparing to share their story with the world while building their future together in the place they both called home.

The first Saturday in December brought the kind of crisp winter morning that made Sweetgum Meadows look like a Christmas card. Demetrius stood at his kitchen window, watching Janelle set up her camera equipment in the backyard, and felt the weight of the ring box in his jacket pocket like a secret that was burning to be revealed. After weeks of planning, today was the day everything would change.

"The light is perfect," she called through the open door, her breath visible in the cold air. She was wearing the soft cream sweater he'd bought her last month, the one that made her skin glow and her eyes look impossibly warm. "Can you bring me that reflector from the dining room?"

He grabbed the equipment and joined her outside, taking a moment to simply watch her work. Six months ago, she'd been a desperate stranger with borrowed equipment and dwindling hope. Now she moved with quiet confidence, arranging her shots with the expertise of someone who had found both her voice and her home. The documentary that had brought them together was finally ready for completion.

"Who's your last interview with?" he asked, though he already knew the answer. They'd planned this moment together, though she didn't know about the additional plans he'd made for afterward.

"You," she said, looking up from her camera with a smile that still made his heart skip. "The story began with Harold's collection, but it's really about what happens when communities commit to preserving and sharing stories that reflect their highest values. You've been the guardian of that vision here."

The morning interview went better than he'd dared hope. Janelle had a gift for making even him comfortable on camera, asking questions that drew out not just facts but emotions, connections, the deeper meaning behind Harold's collection and its impact on their community. When she asked about the moment he'd realized the collection was changing Sweetgum Meadows, he found himself talking not just about Jerome's mentorship program or Tia's writing, but about watching Janelle herself transform from observer to participant.

"It was watching you transition from documenting community to being part of it," he said, looking directly at her rather than the camera. "Showing us what it looks like when someone finds the courage to stop running and start building."

She lowered the camera slightly, caught off guard by the personal turn. "Demetrius..."

"Harold preserved stories about people who used their abilities to build rather than destroy," he continued, his voice growing softer, more intimate despite the rolling camera.

"But you've lived that philosophy. You used your skills to help our community tell its own story, and in the process, you became the heart of what you were documenting."

When they finished filming, the winter sun was beginning to set, painting the sky in shades of orange and pink that looked like a benediction over their work. Demetrius helped her pack the equipment, his hands trembling slightly with anticipation as the moment he'd been planning approached.

"Want to take a walk before dinner?" he asked, trying to keep his voice casual while his heart hammered against his ribs. "The Winter Market opens tonight, and I thought we could get some of Mrs. Zhang's holiday cookies."

"That sounds perfect," Janelle agreed, winding cables with practiced efficiency. "I can't believe the documentary is actually finished. Six months ago, I had no idea this story would become what it has."

They walked hand in hand toward the town square, where vendors were setting up for Sweetgum Meadows' beloved Winter Market. Demetrius had spent weeks coordinating with Mrs. Washington to ensure everything would be perfect—the timing, the lighting, the subtle presence of their community to witness this moment. The square had been transformed with thousands of twinkling lights, garlands of evergreen, and the magical Winter Village that made the space feel like something out of a fairy tale.

"It's beautiful," Janelle breathed, squeezing his hand as they approached the gazebo, which had been decorated with white lights and red ribbons. "Mrs. Washington outdid herself this year."

"She had some extra motivation," Demetrius said, his voice catching slightly.

They paused near the gazebo, where the soft glow of lights created an intimate pool of warmth in the winter evening. Janelle was looking around at the decorations, at their community preparing for the market, completely unaware that this moment had been orchestrated just for her.

"Janelle," he said softly, and something in his tone made her turn to face him fully.

"What is it?" she asked, her eyes searching his face.

This was it. The moment he'd been dreaming about for months, planning for weeks, rehearsing in his mind until every word felt like a prayer. He reached into his jacket pocket, his fingers closing around the ring box as his heart raced.

"Six months ago, a desperate, brilliant woman drove eight hours to Memphis based on a stranger's phone call," he began, his voice steady despite the emotions flooding through him. "She was running from disappointment, from loss, from the fear that she'd never find where she belonged."

Janelle's eyes widened as understanding began to dawn.

"That woman saved Harold's collection, but more than that, she saved me," he continued, pulling out the ring box but not yet opening it. "She taught me that love isn't about choosing between caring for one person and caring for a community. She showed me that the best kind of love makes both stronger."

"Demetrius," she whispered, her hands flying to her mouth.

"Harold's collection brought you to Sweetgum Meadows," he said, dropping to one knee right there in the glow of the holiday lights, "but you chose to stay because you found home here. You chose to build a life with me, with this community, with people who love you exactly as you are."

He opened the box to reveal the vintage ring he'd spent weeks choosing—a classic solitaire with a stone that caught and reflected the lights around them, elegant and timeless like the love they'd built together.

"I love you for your courage," he said, looking up at her face, which was radiant with tears and joy in the soft light. "I love your dedication to authentic storytelling, the way you've helped our community see itself more clearly. I love the life we've built together, and I want to keep building it for the rest of our lives."

Janelle was crying now, the kind of happy tears that made her more beautiful rather than less, and he could hear the soft murmur of their friends and neighbors who had gathered at a respectful distance to witness this moment.

"You made me believe in forever," he continued, his own voice thick with emotion. "You made me understand that the right person doesn't make you choose between love and purpose—they become part of both. Janelle Brooks, will you marry me?"

"Yes," she whispered, then louder as joy overtook her shock, "Yes, of course, yes, always yes!"

His hands were shaking as he slipped the ring onto her finger, and then she was pulling him to his feet, throwing her arms around his neck as applause erupted from the gathering crowd. He lifted her off her feet, spinning her around in the glow of a thousand lights while their community cheered and Mrs. Washington dabbed at her eyes with a handkerchief.

"I love you," Janelle said against his ear, and he could feel her trembling with emotion. "I love you so much, and yes, I will marry you, and build a life with you, and choose you every day for the rest of my life."

When he set her down, she immediately looked at her left hand, where the ring caught the light and sparkled like a promise made manifest. "It's perfect," she breathed. "How did you know exactly what I'd want?"

"Mrs. Zhang may have helped," he admitted with a grin. "And Mrs. Washington. And Jerome. Actually, half the town has been involved in planning this."

As if summoned by his words, their friends and neighbors emerged from their positions around the square. Mrs. Washington appeared with champagne that had materialized from somewhere, Mrs. Zhang carried a tray of celebration cookies, and Jerome approached with his phone ready to capture the moment.

"Did you think I'd propose without the community here to celebrate with us?" Demetrius asked, pulling her close as their people surrounded them with love and congratulations.

"You planned all of this," she laughed through her tears, gesturing at the perfect setup, the timing, the presence of everyone they cared about. "The interview timing, the walk, everything."

"I wanted our engagement to happen in the heart of our community," he said, cupping her face gently while lights twinkled around them like stars. "Surrounded by the people who've watched us fall in love, who've supported us, who've become our family. Harold's stories taught us that the best heroes are the ones who build things with other people. I want to spend the rest of my life building things with you."

The impromptu celebration that followed was everything he'd hoped for and more. Sean appeared with his portable sound system, transforming the Winter Village into their private dance floor. Mrs. Zhang produced more food from seemingly thin air, and someone had arranged for hot chocolate and warm cider to appear as the December evening grew colder.

"Dance with me," Demetrius said, extending his hand to his fiancée—his fiancée—as Sean cued up their song.

They swayed together in the middle of the Winter Village while their community celebrated around them, the holiday lights creating a warm cocoon of intimacy even in the crowd. Janelle fit perfectly in his arms, her head tucked against his shoulder, her left hand resting on his chest where the ring caught the light every time she moved.

"I can't believe you coordinated all of this," she murmured against his neck, sending shivers through him that had nothing to do with the cold. "When did you start planning?"

"The moment I knew I wanted to marry you," he said honestly. "Which was about two weeks after Harold's memorial, if I'm being completely honest. But I wanted everything to be perfect. The documentary finished, you settled in your career, the moment when you'd know with absolute certainty that this is where you belong."

"I've known that for months," she said, pulling back to look at him with eyes that held their entire future. "But this... this is perfect. You're perfect. This community, this life we're building—it's everything I never let myself dream of having."

"And now it's ours," he said, spinning her gently as the music swelled around them.

They danced until the December cold drove most people indoors, though the Winter Market had officially opened around their celebration and families were browsing the stalls with hot chocolate and warm smiles. As they finally walked home through streets that sparkled with holiday lights, Janelle kept stopping to look at her ring, to process the reality of their engagement.

"When?" she asked as they reached their front porch.

"When what?"

"When do you want to get married?"

Demetrius considered the question, though he'd been thinking about it for weeks. "Spring, maybe? April or May, when everything's blooming and beautiful. After the documentary airs and you've had time to enjoy its success. I want to marry you when you can focus completely on us, on our celebration, on the promises we're making."

"Spring sounds perfect," Janelle agreed, leaning against him on the porch they'd painted together last month. "And Demetrius? I want the wedding to be here. In Sweetgum Meadows, with all of this." She gestured toward the town that sparkled with lights, toward the community that had become their family, toward the life they'd built together.

"I wouldn't want it anywhere else," he said, unlocking the door to the house they'd made their own.

Inside, the warmth enveloped them as they shed their coats and moved through the familiar rhythms of home. But everything felt different now, charged with the electricity of their new status, the weight of promises made and accepted.

"Come here," Janelle said softly, taking his hand and leading him to their living room, where they'd spent countless evenings planning her documentary, discussing Harold's collection, building the foundation of their life together.

She turned to face him, her hands coming up to frame his face, the ring glinting in the soft lamplight. "I need you to know something," she said seriously. "Before tonight, before this beautiful proposal, before any of this—I was already yours. Completely. Forever."

"Janelle," he started, but she pressed her fingers gently to his lips.

"Let me finish," she said with a smile. "You gave me everything tonight—the perfect proposal, our community's blessing, this beautiful ring, the promise of a future together. But you'd already given me the most important thing months ago."

"What's that?"

"A home," she said simply. "Not just this house, not just this town, but the feeling of being chosen, of being wanted exactly as I am, of belonging somewhere completely. You gave me the courage to stop running and start building something lasting."

He pulled her closer, overwhelmed by the depth of emotion in her voice, by the certainty and love shining in her eyes. "You gave me that too," he said softly. "You taught me that loving one person deeply doesn't mean loving the community less—it means loving both more fully."

When he kissed her, it was with the passion of six months of growing love and the promise of decades more to come. She melted against him, her hands fisting in his shirt, and he could taste joy and tears and forever on her lips.

"Mrs. Lakeson," he murmured against her mouth, testing how the name sounded.

"I like that," she whispered back. "I like it very much."

They spent the evening calling their families with the news—his sister screaming with excitement in Atlanta, her former foster family the Hendersons crying happy tears when she called to share her joy with the people who had first shown her what family could look like. Each call was another thread binding their separate histories into their shared future.

Later, as they lay entwined in their bed, Janelle traced patterns on his chest while her ring caught the moonlight streaming through their bedroom window.

"Harold would have loved this," she said quietly. "Seeing his collection bring us together, watching it help build something beautiful."

"He would have been proud of more than just his collection's impact," Demetrius said, pressing a kiss to the top of her head. "He would have been proud to see two people use their abilities—for storytelling, for community building, for loving well—to create something that makes the world a little better."

"Speaking of which," Janelle said, propping herself up on her elbow to look at him, "I got a call yesterday from the Network. They want to air the documentary as a special presentation, and they're interested in discussing more projects. Stories about communities that are preserving culture while building something new."

"That's incredible," he said, genuinely thrilled for her success. "You're going to be able to tell stories that matter to audiences who need to hear them."

"We're going to tell those stories," she corrected. "This documentary wouldn't exist without you, without this community, without Harold's collection. Whatever comes next, we build it together."

As she settled back against him, her left hand resting on his chest where the ring caught the light every time she breathed, Demetrius realized that Harold would have understood exactly what they'd created. They weren't just two people who had fallen in love—they were partners who had used their individual abilities to build something that served their community, preserved important stories, and created a love that made everyone around them stronger.

The documentary was complete, the proposal was perfect, and their future stretched ahead of them bright with possibility. Tomorrow would bring wedding planning, career decisions, and all the beautiful mundane details of building a life together. Tonight was for celebrating the end of one story and the beginning of another, wrapped in each other's arms in the home they'd made together, in the community that had made it all possible.

Harold's collection had brought them together, but what they'd built was entirely their own—a love story grounded in shared values, nurtured by community support, and committed to the kind of constructive heroism that created lasting change in the world.

EPILOGUE

*O*ne Year Later

The May morning sun streamed through the windows of the Sweetgum Meadows Community Center, illuminating the woman in the flowing ivory dress who stood before the full-length mirror, adjusting her simple pearl earrings with trembling fingers. Janelle Lakeson—in just a few hours, she would finally be Janelle Lakeson—could hardly believe that her wedding day had arrived.

"Stop fidgeting with those earrings," Nevaeh said with gentle authority, approaching with a steaming cup of chamomile tea. "You look absolutely radiant."

"I can't help it," Janelle laughed, accepting the tea gratefully. "I keep thinking I'm going to wake up and discover this is all some elaborate dream."

The past year had been a whirlwind of success beyond her wildest imagination. Her documentary, "Stories of Hope: How One Man's Vision Transformed a Community," had premiered on the Documentary Channel to critical acclaim and audience enthusiasm. The network had immediately commissioned her to create a series exploring communities across America that were preserving culture while building inclusive futures. She'd been invited to film festivals, interviewed on morning shows, and profiled in journalism magazines as an emerging voice in authentic cultural storytelling.

But more than any professional accolade, the response from communities like Sweetgum Meadows had meant everything. She'd received hundreds of letters from viewers who had been inspired to document their own community stories, to preserve family traditions, to seek out the constructive heroism in their daily lives. Harold's vision had reached far beyond the borders of their small Georgia town.

"The documentary has been nominated for another award," Mrs. Washington announced, entering the bridal preparation room with her arms full of flowers. "Mrs. Zhang just heard it on the radio. Some kind of cultural preservation recognition."

"That's wonderful," Janelle said, though her mind was entirely focused on the ceremony that would take place in two hours. Awards and recognition felt distant compared to the reality of marrying the man who had helped her discover what home could feel like.

Through the community center's windows, she could see the town square being transformed into a wedding venue. White chairs were arranged in neat rows facing the gazebo, which had been decorated with cascades of spring flowers—dogwood blossoms, azaleas, and the sweet-smelling honeysuckle that grew wild throughout Sweetgum Meadows. String lights had been woven through the trees, ready to create magic when evening fell and the reception began.

"How's our groom doing?" asked Mrs. Zhang, appearing in the doorway with a knowing smile.

"Demetrius is pacing in the comic store like a caged tiger," Jerome reported, grinning as he peeked into the room. "He keeps reorganizing Harold's collection displays, which is what he does when he's nervous. Mr. Peterson finally told him to stop touching things before he wore a path in the floor."

Janelle's heart fluttered with affection. Even on their wedding day, Demetrius was taking care of the collection that had brought them together. Harold's Heroes Book Club had grown to over thirty regular members, and the store had become such a community hub that the town council was considering expanding it into the adjacent building. The legacy Harold had hoped for was thriving beyond anything he could have imagined.

"Time for the dress," Nevaeh announced, approaching the garment bag that hung in the corner like a promise waiting to be fulfilled.

The dress had been Janelle's one indulgence in wedding planning—a flowing A-line gown with delicate lace sleeves and a train that would photograph beautifully against the natural backdrop of their outdoor ceremony. When she'd tried it on at the boutique in Atlanta, she'd known immediately it was perfect: elegant but not pretentious, romantic but not overwrought, exactly like the love story she and Demetrius had built together.

As her friends helped her into the gown, carefully buttoning the dozens of tiny pearl buttons up the back, Janelle found herself thinking about the journey that had led to this moment. Two years ago, she'd been a failed documentarian living in her van, desperate enough to drive eight hours on a stranger's phone call. Today, she was about to marry the love of her life in a community that had become her chosen family, with a career built on telling stories that mattered.

"Oh, honey," Mrs. Washington breathed, pressing her hands to her heart as Janelle turned to face the mirror. "You are absolutely stunning."

The reflection that looked back at her was barely recognizable as the scared, desperate woman who had first arrived in Sweetgum Meadows. This woman glowed with happiness and confidence, surrounded by people who loved her, about to pledge her life to a man who had seen her potential even when she couldn't see it herself.

"I have something for you," Tia announced, appearing in the doorway with a small wrapped box. At ten years old, she had appointed herself junior wedding coordinator and had been bustling around all morning with the importance of someone who took her responsibilities very seriously.

Inside the box was a delicate bracelet made of tiny freshwater pearls interspersed with small silver charms—a camera, a book, a heart, and a tiny comic book that made Janelle's eyes fill with tears.

"I made it myself," Tia said proudly. "The charms represent your story. The camera for your documentaries, the book for all the stories you tell, the heart for love, and the comic book for Mr. Harold and how he brought you and Mr. D together."

"Tia, this is the most beautiful gift I've ever received," Janelle managed, her voice thick with emotion as Nevaeh fastened the bracelet around her wrist.

"Don't you dare cry and ruin your makeup," Mrs. Zhang warned, though her own eyes were suspiciously bright. "We have a wedding to get to."

A soft knock at the door interrupted the moment,

followed by Benjamin Walters' gentle voice. "Ladies, I hate to interrupt, but the officiant from the Baptist church has arrived and would like to confirm the ceremony details with the bride."

The door opened to reveal Pastor Williams, the elderly minister who had agreed to perform their ceremony. He was a kind man with gentle eyes who had taken the time to meet with them several times over the past few months, helping them craft a ceremony that felt meaningful and personal.

"Time to go," Jerome announced, appearing with a boutonniere in his lapel and pride written across his face. Since Janelle had no father to walk her down the aisle, she'd asked Jerome to do the honor. The teenager who had helped her understand Harold's collection would now help her begin the next chapter of her story.

The short walk from the community center to the town square felt like floating. The afternoon was perfect—warm but not hot, with a gentle breeze that rustled the dogwood petals and carried the scent of honeysuckle. Every person they passed waved and called out congratulations. Mrs. Peterson paused her gardening to blow them a kiss. The teenagers from Sean's dance studio cheered from the steps of the studio. Even visitors in town for the weekend stopped to admire the bride and her unconventional wedding party.

As they approached the town square, Janelle could see that what felt like the entire population of Sweetgum Meadows had gathered for the ceremony. The white chairs were filled with faces she'd come to love over the past two years—customers from the comic store, members of the book club, fellow business owners, families whose children had been touched by Harold's collection. At the back, she spotted her documentary crew, who had insisted on filming the wedding as a gift to the couple.

But her eyes went immediately to the front of the ceremony space, where Demetrius stood beside the gazebo in a navy suit that made him look impossibly handsome. When he saw her approaching, his face transformed with a smile so radiant that she felt her heart skip several beats. This was the man who had helped her discover what belonging felt like, who had shown her that love could be both passionate and peaceful, who had built a life with her that was everything she'd never dared to hope for.

Pastor Williams, who was serving as officiant, stood ready beside the flower-adorned gazebo. The string quartet from the high school was playing something soft and romantic. Everything was perfect, exactly as they'd planned and dreamed.

"Ready?" Jerome asked, offering her his arm as they reached the beginning of the aisle.

"Ready," she confirmed, though her heart was beating so fast she wondered if everyone could hear it.

The music shifted to Pachelbel's Canon, and the gathered community rose to their feet as she began her walk toward forever. Each step felt momentous, each face in the crowd a testament to the life she'd built in this place. Mrs. Washington dabbed her eyes with a handkerchief. Mrs. Zhang beamed with maternal pride. The teenagers from the store whooped with enthusiasm until Mrs. Peterson shushed them with fond exasperation.

But Demetrius commanded all her attention. He watched her approach with such love and reverence that she felt beautiful beyond description. When she reached the front and Jerome placed her hand in Demetrius's, the rightness of it overwhelmed her. This was exactly where she was meant to be, exactly who she was meant to be with.

"You look incredible," Demetrius murmured, his voice rough with emotion.

"So do you," she whispered back, noting how his hands trembled slightly as he held hers.

Pastor Williams cleared his throat with a warm smile that suggested he was honored to be performing this beloved community ceremony. "Dearly beloved, we are gathered here today to witness the union of Janelle Brooks and Demetrius Lakeson, two people who found each other through Harold Murphy's comic book collection and chose to build something beautiful together."

A ripple of fond laughter went through the crowd. Everyone in Sweetgum Meadows knew their origin story.

"Before we begin the formal ceremony," Pastor Williams continued, "Janelle and Demetrius have asked me to acknowledge the person who made their meeting possible. Harold Murphy believed that stories had the power to change lives, and his collection brought these two together in the most unexpected way. His legacy lives on not just in the comics he preserved, but in the love story he helped create."

Janelle felt tears prick her eyes as she thought about Harold, who had trusted them with his life's work and set in motion everything that led to this moment. She squeezed Demetrius's hands, knowing he was thinking the same thing.

"The couple has written their own vows," Pastor Williams announced. "Demetrius, you may begin."

Demetrius took a deep breath, his eyes never leaving her face. "Janelle, when you first walked into my store, you were looking for a business partner to help you convince a dying man to trust you with his most precious possession. I was looking for someone who understood that comics could be more than entertainment—that they could be instruments of hope and change."

His voice grew stronger, more confident as he continued. "What we found was so much more than either of us was looking for. You taught me that love doesn't mean choosing between caring for one person and caring for a community. You showed me that the right partner makes both kinds of love stronger, deeper, more meaningful."

Janelle's heart felt so full she thought it might burst.

"You took every risk that terrified you," he continued. "You stayed when staying felt impossible. You chose belonging when belonging felt dangerous. You built a life with me when building anything felt like the ultimate vulnerability. Today, I'm promising to spend the rest of my life being worthy of those choices."

His voice caught with emotion. "I promise to love you when you're confident and when you're scared. I promise to support your dreams even when they take you far from home, and to make sure home is always here waiting when you return. I promise to build a life with you that honors both our individual gifts and our shared commitment to serving something larger than ourselves."

He paused, his thumbs brushing across her knuckles. "Harold's collection taught us that the best heroes are the ones who use their powers to build rather than destroy. I promise to spend every day of our marriage building something beautiful with you—a love that makes our community stronger, stories that need to be told, a legacy that makes the world a little better."

By the time he finished, Janelle was crying openly, no longer caring about her makeup. These were the words she'd been waiting her whole life to hear, the promises that made forever feel not just possible but inevitable.

"Janelle," Sean prompted gently.

She took a shaky breath, looking into the eyes of the man who had shown her what home could feel like. "Demetrius, I came to Sweetgum Meadows running from every disappointment and failure in my professional life. I was broke, desperate, and convinced that I didn't deserve the kind of belonging I'd spent years documenting in other people's communities."

The crowd was completely silent, hanging on every word.

"You saw something in me that I couldn't see in myself," she continued, her voice growing stronger. "Not just potential, but worthiness. You didn't try to fix me or save me—you simply loved me exactly as I was while helping me discover who I could become."

She squeezed his hands, grounding herself in his solid presence. "You taught me that home isn't a place—it's the person who chooses you every day, who supports your dreams and shares your values, who builds something meaningful with you that neither of you could create alone."

Her voice caught with emotion. "I promise to choose you every day for the rest of my life. I promise to support your work even when it means sharing you with this community that loves you so much. I promise to use my gifts to tell stories that matter, to preserve the kind of hope Harold believed in, to help other people find the belonging we've found together."

She looked out at the crowd of faces that had become her chosen family. "I promise to be worthy of this community that welcomed a broken stranger and helped her become whole. And I promise to love you with the same constructive heroism Harold wrote about—love that builds, love that heals, love that makes everything it touches stronger and more beautiful."

When she finished, there wasn't a dry eye in the crowd. Mrs. Washington was openly weeping into her handkerchief. Even Jerome looked suspiciously emotional.

"The rings," Pastor Williams announced, and Tia stepped forward proudly, carrying the pillow with their wedding bands.

The rings themselves were simple gold bands that they'd chosen together—elegant, timeless, the kind that would look as perfect in fifty years as they did today. As they slipped them onto each other's fingers, Janelle felt the weight of commitment, the joy of promises made and accepted.

"By the power vested in me by the state of Georgia and this community that loves you both," Pastor Williams said with a warm smile, "I now pronounce you husband and wife. Demetrius, you may kiss your bride."

The kiss was everything their first kiss had been and more—passionate but tender, private despite the crowd, full of love and promise and the joy of knowing they belonged to each other completely. When they broke apart, the crowd erupted in cheers and applause that could probably be heard three towns over.

"Ladies and gentlemen," Pastor Williams announced over the celebration, "I present to you Mr. and Mrs. Lakeson!"

Hand in hand, they walked back down the aisle as rose petals fell like snow around them, thrown by the children who had been waiting for this moment with barely contained excitement. Jerome high-fived random people in the crowd. Mrs. Zhang was taking pictures with three different cameras. Tia was jumping up and down with pure joy.

The reception that followed was everything they'd dreamed of and more. Tables had been set up throughout the town square, decorated with mason jars full of wildflowers and strings of lights that created magic as the sun set. Mrs. Washington had coordinated a potluck feast that showcased the best of Southern hospitality—fried chicken, cornbread, collard greens, sweet tea, and desserts that could have fed twice the crowd.

The first dance was performed right there in the town square, with Sean providing the music from his dance studio equipment and half the town serving as their audience. As they swayed together to their song—the same one they'd danced to at the community celebration after Harold's memorial—Janelle felt overwhelmed by the perfect rightness of the moment.

"How does it feel to be Mrs. Lakeson?" Demetrius murmured against her ear.

"Like coming home," she said simply. "Like everything I never knew I was looking for."

The evening continued with dancing, laughter, and celebration that epitomized everything wonderful about small-town community life. The teenagers from Sean's dance studio performed a choreographed routine they'd created as a wedding gift. Mrs. Peterson surprised everyone by singing a beautiful rendition of their favorite love song. Even some visitors who had been passing through town joined the celebration, drawn by the music and joy that spilled out from the town square.

As the night wound down and the last guests reluctantly headed home, Janelle and Demetrius found themselves alone in the town square, surrounded by the remnants of their perfect day. The string lights still twinkled overhead, and the scent of honeysuckle drifted on the warm evening breeze.

"We did it," she said softly, leaning against him as they looked at their community, their home, the place where they'd built their love story.

"We did," he agreed, pressing a kiss to the top of her head. "How do you feel about forever?"

"With you? Forever isn't nearly long enough."

They stood together in comfortable silence, processing the magnitude of the day, the beauty of the celebration, the weight of the promises they'd made. Tomorrow they would leave for their honeymoon—two weeks in Ireland, visiting the places that had inspired some of their favorite stories. But eventually, they would come back here, to this community that had made their love possible, to the life they'd built together, to the work that gave their partnership meaning.

"Harold would have loved this," Janelle said eventually.

"He would have been proud," Demetrius agreed. "Not just of what his collection accomplished, but of what we built together because of it."

In the distance, they could see the lights of Nerd Central Comics, where Harold's collection continued to inspire young readers, where the book club met weekly to discuss stories of constructive heroism, where their love story had begun with a desperate partnership and grown into something that had transformed them both.

"Ready to go home, Mrs. Lakeson?" Demetrius asked, offering her his arm.

"Ready, Mr. Lakeson," she replied, and they walked together toward their house, their future, their forever—two people who had used their abilities to build something beautiful, exactly as Harold's heroes had always done.

Behind them, the town square settled into peaceful quiet, the string lights twinkling like stars over the place where two strangers had become partners, partners had become lovers, and lovers had become family. In a few hours, the sun would rise on their first day as a married couple, and their real adventure would begin.

But that's a story for another day. Tonight was for celebration, for gratitude, for the perfect end of one chapter and the beautiful beginning of another, in the small Georgia town of Sweetgum Meadows that had taught them both what home could feel like when you were brave enough to stop running and start building something that could last.

AUTHOR'S NOTE

Thank you so much for reading Drawn to You, the fifteenth book in the Sweetgum Meadows Romance series of stand-alone novels. I really hope you loved it! If you enjoyed this book, please consider leaving a review so that others may also find it. Also, if you haven't read the first books yet, check them out today! Although these are stand-alone novels, the stories all intertwine and progress.

I look forward to introducing you to the other characters in this lovely, family-oriented town where each couple will find their happily ever after.

Would you like to receive bonus scenes and keep up with what's next with my upcoming books? Then, make sure you sign up for my mailing list on my website by visiting Imani-Price.com.

Book 1: Love Between Us

Book 2: Sweet Sunsets

Book 3: Infinite Kiss

Book 4: Dance With Me

Book 5: In Charge

Book 6: Forever With You

Book 7: Secret Sweethearts

Book 8: Endless Love

Book 9: The Harder We Fall

Book 10: Reservations of the Heart

Book 11: Play by Play

Book 12: Guarded Hearts

Book 13: Healing Hearts

Book 14: Dear Sweetgum

Novella: Lanterns of the Meadows

Book 15: Drawn to You

Book 16: Under the Sweetgum Tree

Sweetgum Meadows' Visitor's Guide

To all my lovely readers,

Thank you for reading